"You don't
you wan...

Kristy's voice ... ... continued.
"You're just a middle-aged chauvinist who's
bored with life, looking for a new
distraction."

"Putting a label on me may make you feel
better, but it won't stop me," said Blake, a
smile forming on his lips.

"You mean you're going to pursue me
regardless of my wishes? Don't be an
idiot."

"I've dreamed of you, Kristy." His hand
caressed her back, her shoulders, and
threaded through her hair. "You've been
haunting me for years and now you're
going to marry me."

"You're twelve years too late, Blake. I don't
want to marry you, or anyone for that
matter."

His hand moved suggestively against her
hip. "A year from now," he said, "you'll
be my wife. So you can stop worrying about
this job. You won't need it."

Vanessa Grant started writing her first romance at the age of twelve and hasn't forgotten the excitement of having a love story come to life on paper. Currently she teaches business at a community college, but she and her husband are refitting the forty-six-foot yacht they live on with their sons for a world cruise some time in the future. Vanessa believes in love. "After all," she confides, "the most exciting love story I know of is my own."

Books by Vanessa Grant

HARLEQUIN PRESENTS
895—STORM

The Chauvinist
Vanessa Grant

Harlequin Books

TORONTO • NEW YORK • LONDON
AMSTERDAM • PARIS • SYDNEY • HAMBURG
STOCKHOLM • ATHENS • TOKYO • MILAN

Original hardcover edition published in 1987
by Mills & Boon Limited

ISBN 0-373-02888-1

Harlequin Romance first edition February 1988

This Book is Dedicated

to

The Crew of Tarka—Gerry and Janet—
with thanks for the story idea

and, of course,

to Brian
for everything

CHAPTER ONE

BLAKE HARDING scowled at the book in his hands. A spy thriller. He had bought it in Vancouver last summer, picked it up in a drugstore just before he and his mother flew out to the summer home on Saltspring Island. It had disappeared before he got around to reading it. Tonight, a year later, he'd found it resting innocently on the bookshelf, as if it had been there all along.

The book was a cliff-hanger from the start. The hero was immediately thrown into hair-raising danger. Blake closed it with a snap, pushed it back on to the shelf and swung his tall body around, striding silently across the carpet towards the window.

'What do you see out there?' His mother's quiet voice hardly disturbed the gentle music her fingers were coaxing from the piano keys.

'Nothing. Only the lights from across the bay.' He tossed back the dark lock of hair that persisted in falling across the forehead. 'I think I'll go out for a walk.'

'You've been restless this summer. You remind me of your father—Elliott always started prowling when he wasn't working on a project. You wouldn't remember that; you were so young when he died.'

Blake smiled tolerantly at his mother. He was thirty-five years old, but his mother was still searching for similarities to the young husband she had lost thirty years ago.

'I've plenty of projects to keep me busy. There's no end of work waiting back at the office. Canning is waiting for the financial forecast for his new shopping centre, and I've been asked to set up a new information system for the Emerson——'

'I'm not talking about work! I know you enjoy managing the finances of half of Vancouver, but I don't believe you're satisfied with your private life! This year, you've stopped laughing—did you realise that? When was the last time you laughed at a challenge? I keep remembering watching you as a very young man, arguing with Kristy Murdock on the veranda. You were laughing at her. She was furious, and you had that devilish glint in your eye, determined to get your own way. I haven't seen you laugh like that in years. It's time you married, Blake. Time you had a wife and family.'

'Have you got a wife picked out for me?'

'Stop teasing, Blake! Brenda——'

'Brenda?' Something flashed in his eyes, reminding her again of the rascal he had been as a boy. 'I've had enough lazing about. I think I'll go back tomorrow. Will you come, or stay here?'

'Oh, I'll come. But really, Blake! Lazing? This was supposed to be your holiday. You've worked yourself silly, repaired everything that couldn't fight back, not to mention all the work you did over at the Murdocks'.'

'Wasted work. Kristy'll never come back. It won't matter to her if the lawn is cut.'

'I miss that child. Remember how——I suppose she's not a child any more. She'd be almost thirty by now.'

For a moment his black eyes were deep and bleak, then he shook off his thoughts. 'Twenty-eight. Next week she'll turn twenty-eight. I think I'll go out for a walk.'

'Shouldn't you take a jacket?'

'It's warm enough.'

Outside, he walked swiftly towards the water, down the gentle slope of the lawn. The faint light from a sliver of moon drew long shadows from the seaplane moored at the wharf.

He'd fly back tomorrow, bury himself in work for another week, escape the growing discontent that had been stalking him recently.

And would he marry Brenda?

Long streamers of light reached across the water from the summer homes on the other side of the bay. A shadow glided silently across the reflections. Mr and Mrs Hankenson, taking their nightly canoe ride.

Two weeks of relaxing had him climbing the walls. Saltspring Island, home of sunshine and seascape. This summer, the old memories were haunting him.

'I'm supposed to be a practical man,' he told the frog that croaked loudly into the darkness. 'But what do I do about this?'

He had tried work. Work at the office, guiding Earl Canning through his latest money-making project. Work here on the island, repairing the leak in the roof, mending the fence that had never kept the neighbours' children away from his mother's kitchen. This year he had overhauled the garden tractor and used it to mow the extensive lawns. When he ran out of little jobs on his own property, he had prowled next door and mended the broken step at the back of the long-deserted Murdock house, even mowed the lawn.

He had run out of jobs to do.

All day he'd been prowling, thinking, feeling something in the air, as if a storm were building.

'When profits are down,' he explained to the frog, 'you cut costs, try innovations to increase sales. What do you do about this, when satisfaction is down? Yet there's nothing missing.'

He had it all. A successful career, a smoothly

beautiful girlfriend available whenever he called her, a comfortable home—two homes. The official one, presided over by his mother, and the small but well-equipped apartment above his office.

Tame. Too tame.

He laughed, admitting that tonight what he really wanted was a wild young redhead in his arms.

Kristy. She was real enough, or she had been, but she was so far away in both time and distance that he might as well spend his nights wanting the beautiful women on his television screen.

Tonight, she seemed close enough to reach out and touch.

She'd be married by now, spending her days driving her children to school, her nights . . .

Time he had a wife of his own, children of his own.

Brenda would walk through the years with him if he asked her. She would keep everything calm and controlled, just as she kept her smooth, dark hair controlled without any indication of effort.

Kristy's hair had been wild, curling free and uncontrollable. Had she managed to tame the beautiful riot of her red hair with hairdressers' magic?

The house at the top of the slope rested in a dark, ghostly shadow. Except for Blake's recent attention to its needs, no one had been near it in years.

Tonight, the past seemed closer than the present. On the veranda of the darkened house, he could see her ghost, sixteen and incredibly innocent, yet unbelievably desirable in her frothy, low-cut gown. At first she'd been a persistent kid tagging behind him, a young urchin charming him. Then she had begun to change, to show signs of the woman she would be. Against his will, each summer had strengthened the intense longing he felt for her.

Her youth and innocence were more than adequate protection against his desires until that night when, suddenly, she had become a passionate, seductive woman in his arms, driving him to madness . . .

The sound of water brought him abruptly back from the past. It was too early for the Hankensons'. canoe on its way back. He wouldn't have been surprised if a long-necked crane had flown away with a lazy swoop of its wings and a loud, hoarse cry, but there were no cranes, no seabirds of any kind. The ocean glistened smoothly in the moonlight, reflections cutting the darkness with bands of intense light.

A slender arm sliced silently through the water. A gleam of white skin in the moonlight. Her pale back glistened in the soft light, then disappeared in shadows. He stood silently, hardly breathing, listening to the sounds of water as she stood up, half in shadow, emerging from the sea.

Summer after summer, all through his years of high school and university, they had used Kristy's beach as a taking-off point for countless swimming and boating trips, their scantily clad young bodies darkening under the hot sun.

He hadn't seen anyone here in years, hadn't seen either Kristy or her parents since Kristy's sixteenth birthday. This might be a friend they had loaned the summer home to, or perhaps a neighbour out for an ambitious evening swim.

Would his heart pound like this for an anonymous friend of the family? All day, he'd felt——

The damp grass silenced his footsteps.

He watched the sharply defined silhouette as her arms raised. Her hair tumbled half-way down her back as she rubbed it hard with the towel. Her breasts were high and full, her hips flaring from a narrow waist. She wasn't tall, but she moved impatiently, as if she would cover more ground than a girl with longer legs.

She shook her wet hair back, picking up a pair of

jeans and pulling them on while her legs were still damp, struggling and twisting her hips until she had herself zipped in.

As she buttoned a blouse over her bare breasts, he realised his hands were clenched tight against his sides.

It couldn't really be her.

She was moving now, the towel slung over her shoulder, moving out of the light and into the shadow. Blake stepped forward . . .

Kristy had been glorying in the warm darkness, blanketed in solitude. It had been too long since she'd been back to the island; she should have borrowed the cottage long ago. She had needed this—the hot sunshine, the fresh sea wind blowing away the tensions of work. She'd come because her mother asked her to, and because she wanted a chance to organise her thoughts, work out the details of the application she would be handing in on Monday morning.

Director of Business Education at Point Grey College. Was she crazy to believe she had a good chance to get that promotion? She had two counts against her. She was young—under thirty—and she was a woman.

She started up the hill, her mind rushing ahead to a warm mug of chocolate on the veranda, a silent communion with the night to collect her energies for the week ahead.

She would stay until tomorrow night, take the last ferry back to Vancouver.

She heard a sound, like a quickly drawn breath.

'Hello? Is someone there?'

'Sorry. Did I frighten you?'

She couldn't see him yet, but she heard his voice moving closer; it was deeper than she remembered, but with the same warm tones.

'Did I frighten you?' he asked again.

'Hello, Blake.' She caught herself smiling at his dark form, recognising this meeting with the calm inevitability of a dream. She had been thinking of him as she swam, remembering other times when they had raced together in endurance swims across the bay.

She stopped a few feet away from him, shaking her hair to lift the dampness away from her back. The long hair was already starting to curl.

'Kristy?' She felt his fingers against her arm. 'It's been a long time, Kristy. You've grown very beautiful.' The moon slid behind a cloud, leaving only a shadowy glow.

She could barely make out his dark form just inches away from her. If she were beautiful or plain, it would be all the same in this darkness. She remembered the bright beam of moonlight that had guided her to the shore.

'You were watching me dress?'

'I'm sorry.' She heard the thread of laughter under his words.

'You're not a bit sorry.' She laughed with the same reckless confidence he remembered. 'You couldn't have seen much. There's no light at all.'

'Enough to feed my imagination. Where have you been all these years, Kristy? I've been thinking about you tonight, remembering.'

'What were you remembering?'

Their last meeting? But surely, after all these years, it no longer mattered to either of them.

'I remember covering up for you when you threw a baseball through the Hankensons' front window,' he smiled.

'You would remind me of that! I only threw the thing so hard because you said I had a weak pitching arm!'

'Quite true; I provoked you. You're shivering,

Kristy. Come back to our place! We'll find you a hot drink.' His fingers were warm and firm against the damp skin of her upper arm as he urged her up the hill. 'I remember Gary teasing you about jumping in when the rest of us were diving. You cornered me and told me you'd never let me swim on your beach again if I didn't teach you to dive.'

He hadn't changed—he was every bit as attractive as she had remembered.

'It was an advantage, having the best beach around. But you had the best kitchen.'

'Mother's here. She'll be thrilled to see you. We'll——'

'It's far too late. I'll come over in the morning, before I leave.'

'You're leaving already? When did you get here?'

'This afternoon, on the ferry.'

'Didn't you realise we were home? Come over now. You're chilly from the water; a hot drink will set you up.' He had hold of her arm again, was starting to walk the way he wanted to go.

'It's too late, Blake. Your mother——'

'Mother's up, playing the piano. You know what a night owl she is. She was talking about making coffee when I came out.'

'Tomorrow.'

'Tonight. I want you to come tonight. I haven't seen you in years. You can't just pay a quick morning visit and disappear again.'

'Let go!' She tugged her hand away from his, her heart thundering. 'Does anyone ever say no to you, Blake?' In the darkness her voice had a huskiness that she hadn't intended.

'Not often.'

He stopped when she laughed, his hands grasping her shoulders, turning her to him.

'I can't see you at all. What's funny?' His hand

touched her face, as if he could feel the answer with his fingertips.

Her damp curls brushed across his wrist as she shook her head. 'You haven't changed at all, Blake.'

'You've changed. You've grown up, Kristy.'

'I've been grown up for a long time. How's your mother? I haven't heard from her in so long.'

'Twelve years.'

'No. She wrote to me. We corresponded for a while.'

'I didn't know that.'

'I doubt if you thought about me at all. I think Sheila was all you thought about that summer.'

She found her way through the trees on to his grassy lawn where the moon shone. She walked swiftly now, moving towards the lighted window of the Harding house. He lengthened his stride to keep pace.

'When did you come back to the coast, Kristy?'

'Three years ago.'

'You should have called. Why didn't you call?'

'The living-room lights have gone out, Blake. See, there's only one small lamp burning, to light your way back in. Your mom's gone to bed. I told you it was too late.'

'Come in, anyway. She'll have left fresh coffee; we can take it out on the patio and talk.'

'Tomorrow,' she promised.

'You're determined to go?'

'I'm tired. I've been short of sleep lately.'

'Tomorrow, then. But before you go—Kristy, you asked me what I remembered. I've never forgotten your sixteenth birthday.'

'No! It's time you forgot it.'

'You were a child then.' His voice was low, suggestive. His hands found her shoulders in the dark. 'Ever since that night, I've always wondered'—his fingers curved into the bare skin at the tops of her arms—'what it would be like to kiss you when you grew into a woman.'

He was drawing her closer. She could—should —have pulled away from him. Blake Harding was the last man she wanted pursuing her.

He was far too close. His hands slipped down from her shoulders, along the curve of her back. His lips touched hers with an almost electric shock.

Her hands moved against his chest, pushing against the hard muscles.

'Kristy,' he murmured huskily, 'kiss me.'

Just once. Just for a moment. A brief madness in the darkness of a north Pacific island.

She let her fingers spread, feeling the solidness of him through his soft mohair sweater. His mouth searched along the side of her face, pressing soft kisses on her neck, her cheek, her lips.

He grasped her wrists with his fingers, drew them up, placing her arms around his neck. Her fingers found his dark hair.

'No!' She broke away, getting far enough from his hands and lips to regain sanity. For heaven's sake, it was only a kiss, but she was trembling like a young girl!

'What's wrong?'

'It's too late. There's no way——'

'Too late?' He had her shoulders in a swift, tight grip. 'You're not married?'

She twisted away from him. 'No, I'm not married. Let go of me! You and I aren't——'

'Oh yes, we are.' She couldn't see clearly, but she recognised the devilish grin she remembered so well, then his frown as he asked, 'Why do you say it's too late? Are you engaged?'

'You're crazy, Blake. Twelve years is a lifetime—you don't even know who I am any more, if you ever did.'

He let her go, but his voice followed her all the way back to the dark cottage.

'Want to bet, Kristy?' There was laughter in his low voice. 'I'll see you tomorrow.'

No he wouldn't. She make sure of that.

Kristy left on the earliest ferry the next morning.

In the bright, early-morning sunlight, last night seemed impossible. Blake's sudden, determined pursuit of her had surely been a bit of moonlight madness.

If he came for her today, it would be as an old friend, taking her home to visit his mother, remembering old childish pranks. In broad daylight, he wouldn't have the same power to send her heart wild.

There was no danger, no reason not to stay for a morning visit, but she left early, before he would be awake.

She wasn't running; of course she wasn't.

She was remembering his parting comment, his certainty that she would be waiting for him the next day.

No way!

He had had his chance twelve years ago. Kristy wasn't on the market now. If she wanted a man, she'd never choose a sexy male chauvinist like Blake. A man like that would take control of everything; he wasn't taking over even one day of her life!

She slipped silently down the lawn to the dinghy tied at the wharf. She was halfway across the bay when the trees parted to show her Blake's sleeping summer home.

'Serve you right!' she called back, laughing, knowing she'd got the better of him this time. He was probably still asleep, but he'd know when he came knocking on her door. She grinned, knowing he wouldn't be expecting her to disappear like this. People usually did what Blake wanted them to. She always had. Until now.

Summers had been the high point of her young life ever since the year she was ten and her mother had persuaded her father to buy a summer home in the Gulf Islands. Saltspring Island had been everything her mother said it was: a beautiful summer hideaway on the edge of the Pacific Ocean. Vancouver was only a ferry ride away.

For her parents, the cottage had solved the problems of what to do with Kristy during the long holidays. Years ago, they had stopped spending holidays with each other, although they maintained the fiction of a happily married couple until Kristy was sixteen. Summers were the biggest problem, until they bought the cottage. From that time on, Kristy spent her summers on the island, watched over by a series of housekeepers.

She had tagged along with the children from neighbouring summer homes, working hard to earn a place in their group because they were all older than she was. Blake, seventeen and darkly tanned, was their leader, dominating the group with easy good humour.

Once, when she was fourteen, she had seen him blazingly angry. His eyes had been almost the colour of his curly black hair in the instant before he hit Dave Bentley.

That unexplained moment of violence had added a romantic touch of mystery to her dark hero. Blake hadn't explained. Dave, the loser of that brief encounter, had disappeared from their group.

From the beginning, Blake had accepted Kristy's dogging his heels with amused tolerance, treating her with a casual fondness she later recognised as essentially similar to the way her own father had treated her. It meant nothing.

Blake's widowed mother became the anchor of

Kristy's life in the summers. Amanda Harding was a
natural homemaker. She welcomed Kristy into her
kitchen and her home. When the young girl wasn't
swimming and diving with Blake and his friends, she
was learning to cook in the bright kitchen, painstak-
ingly baking a cake and waiting, breathless, for Blake
to approve its taste. Learning to speak gentle gossip
over a hot cup of tea. Awkwardly feeling out the notes
on the Harding piano. On those magical days she felt
wanted and loved, as if she really were a part of this
small family.

The summer Kristy turned fifteen, Blake had been
a sophisticated college student about to graduate.
He'd had a girl that summer. Kristy didn't remember
her name, but that was almost surely a Freudian loss
of memory. She'd been wildly, secretly jealous of the
blonde, full-breasted beauty. Kristy had seen them
from the trees between the two properties, watched
them dancing on the patio to the music of Mrs
Harding's fingers on the piano, then turned away,
knowing that her impromptu visit would not be
welcome. She had gone home to lie alone on her bed
and dream nightmares of Blake pushing her away,
holding the blonde tightly in his arms.

Of course, he had been a natural object for her first
case of hero worship. It was probably inevitable that
she should make a fool of herself the next summer,
trying desperately to show him that she was an attractive woman although she was only sixteen.

And of course, he remembered.

At first, seeing him last night, she had been able to
forget that humiliating scene. He hadn't. He had
remembered, but now he was intrigued.

She was a woman now. Last night, in the moonlight, he'd watched her leaving the water and he had
been aroused, curious. When he reached for her, she
had known an overwhelming desire to know the feel

of his lips on hers again. He'd held her and kissed her as if his life were still his own, committed to no woman. That surprised her, if it was true. Behind his devilish charm she'd always known there was a basic stability; she had seen Blake in her mind as he grew older, inevitably with a wife and children.

Yet last night he had taken her in his arms, kissed her and sent her heart thundering along her veins in a song she denied wanting to hear. As she had moved away from him in the darkness, Blake Harding had let her know in no uncertain terms that he intended pursuing her.

And this morning? What were his thoughts this morning?

She'd give anything to see Blake's face this morning when he found her gone.

It was a foggy morning, chilly enough that Kristy stayed on the ferry deck for only moments before retreating to the warmth of the cafeteria for breakfast and hot coffee.

'Terribly cold for July.'

Kristy looked up at a shapeless cotton coat, unruly grey hair surrounding a lined face. The elderly woman plopped her steaming mug down, then dropped into a too-small chair. She stared expectantly at Kristy.

'It'll warm up once the fog's gone.'

All weekend Kristy had been intending to spend time alone, to think about Jack's resignation and what it could mean to her, how it might affect her relationship with David.

'I'm not ready to think, she decided, settling into conversation, discovering that Ellen Wainright had lived on lighthouses most of her life. She'd been courted as a young girl by a romantic man who rowed ten miles from Victoria to see her each weekend.

Courted. The word had no place in Kristy's modern, practical world. Was that why she felt such a strange fascination with Mrs Wainright's life story?

The Vancouver skyline emerged from the fog shortly before they docked at the ferry terminal. She reclaimed her car from the car park and threaded her way through the heavy Sunday traffic on to the motorway. The sun gained strength as she drove into the city. She arrived home with her windows wide open, her red hair blown into a hopeless tangle.

Her apartment was almost in the heart of the city, tucked into a street that seemed to escape all the roar of traffic and activity. She had been unbelievably lucky to find an empty suite in an old house only two blocks from Kits beach.

Paula was sunbathing on the lawn, looking far too young and happy to be anyone's landlady. Her four-year-old son, Denny, was seated astride her back as if he had found a horse to ride into the Old West.

'You're early, Kristy! I thought you said this afternoon?'

'There wasn't much to do—just look the place over. It was in remarkably good shape considering no one's been near it in years.' Someone had been there, mowed the lawns and replaced two steps with fresh strong cedar.

It must have been Blake.

'Was it hot? It's been scorching here. I've been soaking up the sun, enjoying my days off while Dean slogs over his books.'

'Was there a beach?' asked Denny, staring up at her curiously, his platinum hair tousled wildly across his grubby forehead.

'A nice beach.'

'As big as ours?' Size was important to Denny.

Kristy laughed. 'Not nearly as big as our beach. It was different. Here we share the beach with everybody. There, it's a private beach.'

'No one else can come?'

'Only if they're invited.'

Blake hadn't been invited. He had come anyway.

'You look tired.' Paula shifted to rest her chin on her elbow. 'Why don't you put on a swimsuit and laze about in the sun with me?'

'Maybe later. I've got some marking to do first.'

Upstairs, Kristy went around throwing windows open, starting an electric fan to get the hot air moving. She took a cool shower and brushed her damp curls into submission, then changed into shorts and a brief halterneck top. In the end she took her marking down on to the lawn and tried to assess a confused student's grasp of computer programming while she soaked up the heat and let Denny rescue her from the bad guys of his four-year-old fantasies.

When the phone rang she went tearing up the outside stairs to her living-room, picking up the receiver just in time to hear the dialling tone. Only three rings and the caller had hung up. That would be her mother, too impatient to wait. She'd call again in a minute.

Kristy picked it up on the first ring.

'Where were you a minute ago?'

'Outside, sunbathing.'

'Oh.' Kristy doubted if Stephanie Murdock had ever pursued such a purposeless activity as sunbathing in her life. 'Well, did you get over to the cottage?'

'I just got back this morning. I ran into Blake Harding over there.'

'Did you? What about the place? What kind of shape is it in?'

'Not bad, actually. Are you really going to sell it? You should go and see it first. It's beautiful over there, incredibly——'

'It's useless to me. I don't know why we've kept it all these years, but now that Verne has agreed to sell there's no point delaying. What needs doing before it can go on the market? Did you make a list?'

Kristy had. She read it to her mother, then offered, 'I could do the interior work. I've got holidays coming next month; I'd like to spend them on the island. I could paint the kitchen, do the cleaning up.' Blake would be gone by then. He had the look of a successful businessman; certainly he wouldn't spend the entire summer hidden away on Saltspring Island. Even if he was still there, she would be prepared for the sight of him this time.

'I'll get professionals to do it. Aren't you spending your holiday with David?'

'Part of it, but David's holidays don't start until the last week of August. We'll be going down to San Francisco for a few days.'

'I see,' said her mother dismissively, losing interest. 'About this Wednesday—I'd like you to have lunch with me.'

They talked on the telephone about once a month, but they saw each other less often. Dr Stephanie Murdock's patients left little time for personal contacts, even with her daughter.

'At Manuel's,' her mother decreed. 'That way I can get over to the hospital for my rounds when we're done.'

'All right.' She'd have a twenty-minute drive to get there from the college, but there was no point trying to change her mother's mind. Wednesday's lunch hour would be very rushed.

By the time Kristy got back to the lawn, the sun had disappeared behind a cloud. She collected her marking and went to make supper, writing comments on students' computer printouts as she waited for a frozen TV dinner to cook in the oven.

The phone rang again while she was eating.

'How was your weekend?'

'Hi, David! Not bad, how about yours? How were your daughters?'

'They enjoyed Stanley Park. Frankly, though, I had trouble keeping my mind on them. Luckily they were charmed by the swans on the lagoon. I've been worrying about Jack. How could he just leave us like that, with so little warning?'

'Three months' notice. And how could he refuse Waterloo University? A full professorship!'

'I suppose so, but Lord knows who'll take his place. It would be just our luck to get a new broom as director, some computer whiz kid who'll turn us into the technical marvel of the age. Everything's going computer these days.'

'Maybe I'll apply for Jack's job.' She said it lightly, and she laughed when David did, but she would have her application letter ready by morning.

CHAPTER TWO

By monday morning Point Grey College was buzzing with the news of Jack's resignation. Kristy arrived early and poured herself a cup of coffee in the staff-room, fielding questions from two academic instructors.

'I don't know any more than you do. It was a total surprise to me. Sorry, I've got to get ready for my first class.'

She escaped into the office she shared with Wilma Duncan. Wilma's short blonde hair was already wildly ruffled by her impatient hands as she struggled over a stack of students' papers.

'Would you believe this fellow?' Wilma waved a paper covered with dark, masculine handwriting. 'I ask you! Second year business admin, and the fool doesn't know a floating exchange rate from a sailboat!'

'I bet he'll know the difference by lunchtime.'

'You bet your boots he will!' Wilma scrawled a brief message across the paper in red ink. 'How was your weekend? The Gulf Islands?'

'That's right. Saltspring Island. It was nice—clean air, sunshine. I don't think there's been a breath of change there since I was a teenager. Have you been in the staffroom this morning? Jack's taken them by surprise.'

Wilma laughed, her rough voice booming out. 'I saw him this morning. We walked in from the car park together. After dropping his bombshell, he's suddenly found some conference over in Richmond that'll keep him busy till Wednesday—the coward! He told me he wants to see you before he goes this morning.'

'If I hurry, I can see him before my first class. I'd better go now. Hand me that manual, would you? Yes, that one. See you at coffee break.

'Oh, Kirsty, before you go—David was by a few minutes ago. He said to tell you he had examinations this morning—he'll see you at lunch.'

'OK. If you see him in the cafeteria, tell him I might be a couple of minutes late.'

Jonathan Kinney was leaving Jack's office as Kristy arrived. He glared at her, greeting her with a voice as frosty as his smoothly groomed hair.

'Shut the door, Kirsty,' Jack instructed her. Then, as the door closed. 'I'll swear that man Kinney believes that he's the only one who matters in this department.'

'He's been here longer than any of us.' Kinney taught accounting and tax in Kristy's department. Secretly, she was grateful that they seldom saw each other in the course of a normal day. 'By the way, Jack, congratulations on your new job!'

Jack sat down, managing to look as if he might leap back out of the chair at any moment. He was short, heavily built, but radiating suppressed energy from his polished leather shoes to his bristled dark hair.

'Thanks! Kristy, are you planning to apply for my job?'

'You must be a mindreader. I've got my application here. Who should I give it to? Dr McAllister?'

'I'll take it. There'll be a selection board, of course, but I've been asked to screen the applicants. You've got a very good chance. Your degree from Waterloo carries a lot of weight. The board is very computer-minded these days, and University of Waterloo has a name in that field. And, of course, your work here

—you've started several new courses—that computer certificate programme——'

'Is Jonathan Kinney applying?'

'So he says. That was the purpose of his visit this morning. I doubt if he has a chance, Kristy. The college can't afford a director of business studies who isn't up on modern technology. I can't guarantee you'll get the job either—depends on who else applies—but I can almost guarantee Kinney won't get it.'

'He won't like it if I'm his boss.'

'He didn't like it when I became boss, either. You can handle him. I did.'

Kinney would be watching for her to make a mistake, waiting to carry tales about her to the Principal.

Jack was ticking off people on his fingers. 'Wilma could give you a run, but she doesn't want the job. Too much responsibility. She wants to be able to leave the college behind when she goes home to Jake. There's David, but he's weak on computers. He's a fence-sitter, keeps out of the perpetual feuds around this place, so you won't have any problem with him. David always respects authority, and he has no ambition to have my job.'

Jack spoke as though he were unaware of any personal relationship between Kristy and David. It was his way of telling her that personal matters should have no bearing on her career decisions.

He glanced up from the papers he was shuffling, gave her a quick, sharp look. 'I imagine you're thinking I'm indiscreet, talking so frankly about our colleagues. But I believe you'd do a good job here. And if you do want the job, you'll have to think about politics. Your real problem comes from our Principal. I think Dr McAllister knows women have been let out of the kitchen, but he's not comfortable with the idea.

Anyway, time enough for that later. I need your help, Kristy. Gunnar Gustafsen has thrown a monkey wrench into my night-school schedule.'

'Gunnar? Isn't he teaching the computer applications course at night school? He's a good instructor.'

'He is, but he's pulled out on me. Damn part-time instructors! We need them, but——Gunnar's employer has transferred him to Montreal. He's leaving next week, so he can't teach the course.'

'I don't think I can help you, Jack. I can't think of anyone who could do it.'

'You could do it.'

'I'm already doing one night course—Thursday nights.'

'This one is only a four-week course, one night a week. Saturday labs, but I've got a lab assistant hired for those. All you have to do is Monday nights for four weeks. The course is full. I'd hate to cancel it. The class list is all businessmen, people who've been demanding a course like that for months.'

'Jack, I'd be wiped! Going day and night! I——'

'One of the businessmen who signed up to take it is the newest member of our advisory board. I suspect he's taking the course to check up on us so I don't dare use a green instructor.'

'Who is he?'

'Better you don't know that. Here's the paperwork —class list and Gunnar's outline. The class starts tonight.'

'Tonight! Come on, Jack! How can I be ready for tonight? Why on earth did you tell me about that board member? I'd be better off not knowing he was there!'

'True, but you might have refused to teach the class. Now off you go. You've got a spare period this afternoon. Maybe you can use it to get organised for tonight. If not, you can wing it! I'm sure you could teach this stuff standing on your head.'

Kristy left Jack's office shaking her head, mentally juggling her day in search of a few free moments. The spare period was already spoken for by two students who needed help in computer programming. That left lunchtime.

She spent her lunch hour looking over Gunnar's outline, realising that there was nothing in the course material that would give her a problem. It was always a challenge teaching people who worked with computers on a daily basis, but she felt confident the evening wouldn't bring anything she couldn't handle. Except for the anonymous advisory board member.

Better not think about him. She'd had important people in her night classes before. There was only one way to deal with a situation like that. She had to ignore everything outside the classroom, concentrate on the people in front of her, on their desire to learn. It didn't matter who they were outside the classroom.

After half an hour with Gunnar's notes, she felt confident enough to leave her work and slip over to the cafeteria for a few moments. David was still there, his curly blond head tossed back as he talked eagerly with Wilma about some amusing incident from this morning. Jonathan Kinney was seated at a nearby table, listening to the college bursar with an attentive expression.

'I didn't think you'd be this late,' David greeted her.

'Jack talked me into taking over a night class.'

'Gunnar's?' Wilma shook her head at Kristy. 'I heard he'd been transferred. You're a sucker for punishment, my dear. You should have told Jack to go whistle up a—what do you whistle up? Whistle up the wind? No matter, but do you realise that Gunnar's class starts tonight?'

'I realise.'

Sometimes David frowned in hopes that it would make him look older. This time he was frowning for real.

'Had you forgotten that we were going out tonight, Kristy?'

'I know. I'm sorry, but Jack wasn't taking no for an answer. I'm tied up for the next four Mondays.'

'And Thursdays. With you teaching Monday and Thursday, and me teaching the communication class Tuesdays——Damn! Dinner Wednesday, then?'

'All right. But let's not go out. Teaching nights always exhausts me. By Wednesday I'll be in no shape for a social evening out. Come over to my place; I'll do us a steak. If I'm too tired to cook, I'll order a pizza.'

David's irritation was short-lived. 'OK. I've got a new tape you'll want to hear—I'll bring that along.'

'We must try to get Jack to arrange the schedule better this autumn,' David told her as he walked back with her. 'It would be nice if we both taught the same night. We could have more time together.' He gave her arm a light, inconspicuous squeeze, all he could manage in a corridor filled with alert students.

'Jack will be gone,' she reminded him, moving away towards the computer lab where her class waited.

'Ms Murdock! Can you help me? I can't make those stupid numbers line up—look at the mess on my screen!'

Kristy bent to read the screen, then turned to help a worried elderly man who was making a desperate effort to understand the computer revolution.

Hours later, she found herself driving home just ahead of the rush-hour traffic, her mind spinning in the aftermath of a day filled with students' questions. At work she concentrated every ounce of her energies on the learning process that was happening around her. She loved the job, but she was frequently exhausted by the hectic pace she demanded of herself.

She parked her red car in the drive and ran up the outside stairs to her door. She was on the verge of fatigue, felt she had to keep running to avoid wilting and having to drag herself up the stairs. She couldn't let herself unwind yet. She had that night-school class to get through first.

She kicked off her shoes and stockings, put on a tape of a haunting folk singer to soothe away the tensions as she paced restlessly for a moment, then took a quick shower.

She had an urge to change into jeans and T-shirt as she came out of the steaming bathroom. Not yet. She had to keep up her businesslike image a few more hours.

She ate the rest of last night's salad for supper, eating with the bowl in one hand as she stood on the balcony and looked out over the water.

If she succeeded in her bid for Jack's job, she would be the youngest department head at Point Grey College. If she got the job, she would have to stop seeing David. They were friends. Romantic friends, she thought with a smile. Lately, David had even been hinting at marriage. But whatever the relationship, it couldn't continue once—if—she got the director's job. It would be a definite conflict of interests to be dating one of her own instructors.

Whenever she looked out towards the ocean, she could see the house where David had his apartment. She had told him about that vacant apartment when he first came to the college, and he had leapt at the chance of a comfortable bachelor suite near the beach.

Working together, living in the same neighbour-hood, they had naturally started seeing more of each other. From the beginning they had shared so much—their work, their love of old folk songs, their desire for personal independence.

Kristy had approached their relationship warily, gradually relaxing as she realised that David posed no threat to her independence. If he did get around to asking her to marry him, it would be in cold blood, a rational question asked across a dinner table one night.

She would have her answer ready, too. The same answer she had given the last man who asked. No.

The phone pealed across the early evening air. She moved slowly towards it, stopping first to set her bowl in the sink.

'Hello?'

'Kristy? It's Amanda Harding. Blake tells me I missed you the other night. I'd no idea you were in this part of the world! I thought you were still back east. How are you, my dear?'

'Mrs Harding! It's great to hear your voice again!'

'It's been a long time. Will you come and visit me, Kristy? I'm living in New Westminster. I know it's a bit of a trip from town, but I'd love to have you to dinner. We can catch up on each other over the last few years. Will you come? Tomorrow if you can. Blake has to meet with a client, so it'll be just you and me over dinner and a lengthy session with the coffee pot.'

'I'd love to! Tomorrow's perfect.'

'Do you have a car? If transportation is a problem, Blake could pick you up before he goes out.'

'No!' She realised she sounded panicky, repeated, 'No need for that, I've got a car. Just give me the address and I'll find my way.'

She was still smiling over the thought of dinner with Amanda Harding when she arrived at the college for her night class. It was twelve years since she had seen the older woman, but her voice on the telephone tonight had been as warm and welcoming as Kristy remembered.

And Blake wouldn't be there. Not that it mattered really, but it was nicer to think of having Mrs Harding to herself for the evening.

She shed her coat in the staffroom and went down to unlock the classroom. She was half an hour early, but she found an eager couple already waiting outside the locked classroom.

'Walter Zeigler.' The tall, lean man thrust out a hand towards her, then quickly pulled it back. 'Sorry, your hands are full. Can I take something for you? Oh, this is my wife, Sheila. I'm in life insurance. What happened to the other instructor? Guster?'

Could this be the board member? Possible, but not likely. She said, 'Gustafsen. He's moving to Montreal. Just set the papers down here, on this desk. We won't be starting for a few minutes. If you'd like a cup of coffee, there's a coffee machine in the hallway.'

'Is the coffee in it any good?'

'Frankly, it's terrible. It spits out some mixture of powder and hot water.'

'We'll try it anyway. Thanks.'

The class assembled slowly over the next twenty minutes, people trickling into the room one by one, looking around uncertainly as if for a familiar face. Kristy hadn't looked at the class list yet. The names meant nothing to her until she could put faces to them. She was pleasantly surprised to find one of her ex-students had come back for a refresher course.

'I'm afraid I'll get behind if I don't keep taking courses,' Darren Bailey announced as he walked into the classroom. Several others nodded their agreement of his statement.

Kristy had been perched on a desk, talking to a couple of the students while she waited for the room to fill. The room fell silent now, as she went to the front of the class.

'I think most of you are here, so let's start. Some

of you look surprised to see me here. Your instructor, Gunnar Gustafsen, has been transferred to Montreal and I've been asked to take over. I'm Kristy Murdock.'

Darren smiled at her from a back seat and announced, 'That's good news for me, Ms Murdock. I think you're the best instructor in the college. You always manage to make the most difficult things seem easy.'

'Thanks, Darren.' The door opened as another student slipped silently into the room. 'I'd like to start tonight by finding out a bit about each of you. This is an advanced course, so you'll all have some experience of computers. I expect some of you have quite a bit. I'd like you each to identify yourself, then tell us a bit about your background——' she turned to include the newcomer in her smile, and found her lips freezing, her words growing stilted as she finished, 'and I'd like to know what each of you hopes to get out of this course.'

Blake.

He was motionless, standing with his hand still on the doorknob, his black eyes staring at her. Had he followed her here, or was he as astounded as she was?

Her eyes fell to the class list in her hand. His name was there. She'd swear it was blacker than the others, the words shouting up at her from the page. Blake Harding.

Blake said, 'Have I wandered into the wrong room? Gunnar Gustafsen's class?'

'No. I mean you haven't. Mr Gustafsen wasn't able to——He's had to cancel. I'll be teaching the course instead.'

He was still staring, as if he were waiting for her to say more. She glanced around at the rest of the class, caught Darren's admiring glance and clutched at it like a straw.

'If you'd like to find a seat, Mr Harding, we'll carry

on.' She kept her eyes away from him. Somehow, she'd have to ignore the man. Damn Blake! How could he turn up here in her class? 'I'll start with a familiar face. Darren is an old student of mine. Darren, would you tell us a bit about yourself.'

How could she ignore six feet of muscular, aggressive, sexy Blake? Tune him out?

'Thanks, Darren. Who would like to go next?'

'I will. I'm Delia Devonworth. I work in a doctor's office. We've had computers for a couple of years now, but we've had a lot of problems with them.'

Kristy always liked to get new students talking, relaxed, ready to learn and experiment. She could feel it happening, the group psychology taking hold as these people started sharing their experiences with her, and with each other.

What would Blake have to say? Or would he say anything? He kept watching her. The others looked around, sharing glances with each other. Blake's eyes seemed locked on her face. It was downright unnerving. What would they all think if she suddenly shouted at him to stop staring at her?

'Blake Harding,' he identified himself when his turn came. His voice was deep and confident. 'I'm an accountant with a practice here in Vancouver. I do some management consultations. Of course, these days, that usually means I have to advise my clients on what computer system to use, what software to buy.' He smiled suddenly, a devastating smile that had the woman beside him—Alison, her name was—patting her hair to be sure it was at its man-catching best. 'I'm taking this course in hopes that I'll learn the answers before my clients ask the questions.'

The man behind Blake nodded. Walter Zeigler, the insurance man, looked as if he might try to catch a quiet minute with Blake to ask for some free advice.

'Have I got everyone?' Kristy asked briskly. She

gave a quick glance around the room, mentally putting
names to all the faces.

'Except for you,' Blake challenged her. 'I'm sure
we'd all like to know a bit about your background.'

'Of course. I was getting to that next.' Why should
she sound defensive? She went briefly over her
university background, her years as a programmer in
Toronto, then her appointment to Point Grey College.
Blake should have been impressed by it all—certainly,
some of the others looked impressed. But not Blake.
He had a strange light in his eyes, as if he were just
waiting to get her alone.

'Darren, would you hand these course outlines
around? Does anyone have any other questions? As
you can see from the outlines, we're keeping it very
flexible. No questions? All right, then, let's go down
to the computer lab.' Damn the man. Would he never
stop watching her? 'Tonight I'll do some demonstra-
tions of the software we're using, then I'll send you
off with some homework. Something that relates to
what you're doing in your own offices.'

He wasn't going to stare at her for four weeks of
Mondays. No way. She'd find a way to fix him!

It wasn't long before Kristy had most of them
sitting at the computers. Everyone seemed to enjoy
getting hands on the lab equipment, except Delia, the
medical office worker. Kristy soon had them working
on the beginning of the project that would occupy
their next four weeks.

It was more than half-way through the class before
Kristy had a moment to lean back against one of the
tables and take a deep breath. For a brief moment,
everyone was busy, involved, and none of them needed
her.

'What the devil are you doing here, Kristy?'

She swung around, finding herself close up against

the soft mohair sweater that covered Blake's broad chest.

'Don't sneak up on me like that!' She was whispering, but felt hoarse as if she were shouting. 'You know what I'm doing here. I——'

'Teaching? It doesn't make sense, Kristy. You're a beautiful woman. This is no life——'

'Kristy?' Delia's plaintive voice cut over Blake's low tones. 'I need help. It just doesn't make sense to me.'

'Mr Harding had just finished that section. He'll give you a hand.' She smiled full at Blake and left him there, firmly in the clutches of the bewildered Delia. Much later, she looked across the room and saw that he was still sitting beside Delia, explaining something patiently to her.

Then, suddenly, he looked up and something flashed in the depths of his eyes.

Kristy couldn't help giggling. She wouldn't have any problem keeping her distance from Blake in this classroom. Delia had one hand resting on his arm, her eyes looking up pleadingly.

'I'd like you to work on with the partners you've worked with tonight,' Kristy announced, smiling at the look of alarm in Blake's eyes.

'Hey, Sheila, is this ever something! Miss Murdock—Kristy!' Walter was almost stuttering in his excitement. 'Come and take a look at this! I'm going to turn our office upside down with this program.'

Kristy was busy for the next two hours, but the problem of avoiding Blake was in the back of her mind. When the class ended, he would be waiting. Somehow, she had to avoid being alone with him at the end of the evening.

As she concluded the class, announcing lab times and homework for the next week, she knew exactly what she would do.

'Help me clear up, will you, Darren?'

He was willing, and he knew the routine from his days as her student. He followed her to the storeroom with arms full of manuals and disk boxes. Kristy glanced back and saw Delia moving towards the door with her hand still clutching Blake's sweater, Blake shooting a look back that seemed to promise he'd get her for this.

'How's work going, Darren?'

'Great! I sure appreciate the reference you gave me. I'm sure it got me the job.'

'Hand me that binder—the blue one. Thanks.' She turned the key in the cabinet. 'Are you still living near the beach?'

'Yup. I've got the upstairs room in the same building Mr Roswell lives in.' Kristy nodded. It was Darren who had told her about the vacancy that later became David's home.

'I can give you a ride home if you like.'

'Great! The bus won't come for twenty minutes now. Buses aren't very good this time of night out here. What about this box? Do you want it put away?'

'No, that's just blank disks. Let's check around the computer room, then I'll get my coat and we'll go. If you want to stop by my place next Monday, I could give you a lift to the next class. We live so close.'

'I'll do that. I can give you a hand with anything you want carried, and getting the classroom ready. I'll check the windows. Everyone's gone—oh, there's still —hello, Mr Harding!'

'Blake,' he corrected. He was lounging against the shelf by the window, his hands pushed deep into his pockets. How had he managed to give Delia the slip? 'We've met before, haven't we? You work for Towers? I thought so. We'll be spending the better part of next week together.'

'Yes, I know. Mr Towers assigned me to be sure

you had access to everything you need. I've been looking forward to it for days.'

'I told him to give me his best worker. Where's your coat, Kristy? In the staffroom? That's down this way, isn't it?'

Darren was watching them both curiously, so she could hardly ask Blake why he was hanging around.

Blake smiled at her and said, 'I'll take a ride with you, too, Kristy. I'm on your way. Kits area, didn't you say? My apartment's on Pine Street.'

'Don't you have your own car?'

'I don't care to drive in the city. Public transport's faster, and there are already more than enough cars on the roads in Vancouver.'

'My car's small. You'll be uncomfortable.'

'We'll manage to squeeze in, won't we, Darren?'

'No problem. I'll go in the back.'

'Round two to you,' muttered Kristy. Darren looked blank, but Blake grinned and followed her into the staffroom.

'Why are you following me?'

'Don't you dare stick that Devonworth woman on me again! That was a low trick!'

'Serves you right!'

'Now I wonder why you think that? What are you doing with young Darren? He's far too young for you—he can't be more than twenty and you're almost thirty. Still single, too. How come, Kristy? I'd have expected you to be married with a couple of children by now, not working, living alone.'

'You expected wrong.'

'You are living alone, aren't you? You need a man to take you away from all this.'

She couldn't stop herself from laughing. 'My God, you're ridiculous! Here we are in the nineteen-eighties and you're trying to sell me on the poor-little-woman scene! Move out of the way so I can get my coat, will you! I promised Darren a ride and he's out there in the hallway. He'll be wondering——'

'He won't be wondering. He's an obedient boy, he knows his place. He's a student, so he wouldn't follow us into the staffroom. Which coat? It must be the green one, it couldn't be the red one, not with your hair!'

'Will you shut up about my hair! You've been making cracks about it since I was ten years old!'

'Is this the way you talk to all your students? It seems a bit informal to me.'

She giggled. 'Always. It's part of my style. Dr McAllister, our Principal, comes and sits in on the odd class. When he's there I have to cool it a bit. You should meet him.'

'I have, actually. It wasn't a particularly memorable experience. The man's a bit of an ass.'

'Funny. I was just going to say you've a lot in common with him. He's got the same ideas about women, thinks we should all be tied to a hot stove.'

'And wouldn't you rather have a man and a home to look after, instead of having to drag yourself to work every day, coming home to an empty apartment.'

'You're unbelievable! You——No, this is ridiculous! I've got better things to do than waste time arguing with male chauvinists.' She thrust her arms into her coat and turned off the light, leaving Blake to find his way out of the staffroom in darkness.

Behind her, she heard a thump and a muffled curse—he had collided with the coffee table. She winced. She had hit that table herself more than once. It was massive, carved of dense hardwood.

'Are you ready, Darren? Sorry I was so long.' She avoided looking at Blake as he emerged behind her. Was he limping slightly?

'You would have a red car,' Blake teased her as

they arrived at the small Honda. 'You know it doesn't go with your hair, but you always did have a passion for red.'

Passion. The word fell into the silence in the car park. 'If I can't wear red, at least I can have a red car. Darren, tell me how Marion's doing. I haven't seen her since the wedding.'

'She's fine. She's working now, too, you know. She got a job at the university—temporary, but the experience is good. And she's expecting a baby.'

Blake ended up in the front seat, his arm brushing against her whenever she had to change gear. Kristy set the Honda in motion with a lurch and drove out of the car park. At the stop sign, she pushed the clutch in. The Honda promptly went into a shuddering vibration.

'You should have that fixed,' Blake told her as she waited for a truck to pass before pulling out herself.

'It'll stop in a minute.' She put the little car in motion and the vibration smoothed.

'It's your clutch. It needs adjusting.'

'You're an expert, I suppose. Pine Street, you said?'

'That's right. You can let Darren off first.'

'Much more convenient if I let you off first. Darren lives just a few doors from me. Which way on Pine? Left or right?'

'Left. Pull up behind the red van.'

'That's an office building. Harding and McKay. Is that you? I've driven past here countless times. I've never noticed that sign before.'

'But then, you weren't looking for me, were you?'

'Are you going back to work? This late?'

'No, I've an apartment upstairs.'

'And who's McKay?'

'Norm McKay. We've been partners for seven years now. Are you having dinner with my mother tomorrow night?'

'I——You're not going to be there, are you? Your mother said——'

'I've got a meeting with a client. After the way you dashed off on Sunday morning, I assumed you wouldn't come if I was going to be there. I hope you are going. Mother's really looking forward to it. She's missed you.' He stood leaning into the open doorway on the passenger side of her car, searching her expression with his eyes. 'You are going, aren't you?'

'Yes, I told her I would.'

'Good. So long, Darren. Glad to have met you. Kristy, get that car into the garage tomorrow.'

Bossy, objectionable man. But she was grinning as she drove away. She certainly wasn't going to a garage. If she got pressured into giving him a ride next Monday, she'd make sure he knew she hadn't been to a garage.

She put the car back into gear, glad that Darren was too polite to ask any of the questions that must be in his mind.

All the way home, Darren talked about Blake, singing his praises with second-hand information that he had gleaned from his employer. If she could believe any of it, Blake Harding's guidance was the primary reason for Towers' great success in recent years.

He would be successful. He was entirely too sure of himself. He needed taking down a peg or two, but she doubted if anyone had managed that since she last saw him.

She should be married, keeping house for some man, should she? Damned arrogance! Any more of his nonsense and she'd show him.

She had an effective weapon to use against him. Delia Devonworth.

CHAPTER THREE

BLAKE must have been living nearby ever since she moved in upstairs from Paula and Dean. When she returned to Vancouver, she had known he would be somewhere close, but it was a big city. They could share it for years without seeing each other.

Strange that all those summers when Blake was a university student she had never known, never asked, what he was studying. Of course, he would be an accountant. Just one more thing he shared with her father. Why hadn't *he* married yet?'

Amanda Harding's home was a safe twenty-five miles away in New Westminster. If Blake wasn't married, why didn't he live with his mother? It seemed a pity that such a warm, loving woman should live alone.

Kristy found the house high on a steep hill with an impressive view of the water. She didn't need to look at the number to know it was the right house. Something about the restrained opulence of the old stone and wood residence fitted the Harding family. The house radiated a comfortable stability.

'Kristy!' Mrs Harding drew her into the thickly carpeted hallway with a warm embrace. 'You're looking wonderful, my dear! How are you?'

Kristy couldn't remember ever kissing her own mother, but she felt no discomfort at returning this woman's embrace.

'I'm fine. It's so good to see you! I've wondered——You were next door every summer, but I never saw where you lived the rest of the year.'

43

'My husband bought this place for us the year Blake was born. We were very happy here.' The older woman glanced around, her eyes filled with memories.

She was older, of course. On Kristy's sixteenth birthday her eyes had been a deeper blue as she handed Kristy a card with the New Westminster address, insisting that Kristy write from Toronto. In the years since, her greying hair had turned completely white. Her smile now brought deeper lines to her face, but the warmth hadn't dimmed. The face reflected its owner's youthful approach to life.

'You must call me Amanda. You're not a child now. Come into the living-room. We'll have a glass of wine before we eat. I was so disappointed to miss you the other night at the island.'

'Blake wanted me to come in, but your lights were out. It was late.'

'Blake said you'd be over the next morning.'

'Yes, well—I had to get back, had to catch the early ferry. I only went to check on the house for Mother.'

'Blake went over the next morning to bring you back for breakfast. He was quite put out to find you gone. He was like a bear with a sore head at breakfast that morning.'

'Was he?' She couldn't help a slight smile.

'It probably served him right,' Amanda observed in a disconcerting reflection of Kristy's own thoughts. 'I suspected you two had been arguing. Now tell me about yourself. You went to Toronto with your father. You wrote me for a couple of years—cheerful letters that made me suspect you were having a miserable time.'

'I suppose everyone goes through a bad time in those teenage years.'

'You stayed with your father how long?' Amanda's face hardened as she remembered a young Kristy leaving Saltspring Island, hanging on her father's arm in ignorance of the impatience that flashed in his cold blue eyes.

'Just a year. I went to university when I was seventeen, lived in residence there.' She could have commuted, could have remained living with her father smiling falsely for his latest woman, playing hostess for business dinners in the intervals between his girlfriends.

'I took a degree in computer science, then I worked as a programmer for a software house in Toronto until I decided to go back to university for graduate studies. Once I had my master's degree, I went back to work for the same place, doing system analysis —figuring out what clients needed for computer equipment, setting up new systems. That was fun, but I really wanted to get back to the west, so I applied for a teaching job at Point Grey College. I've been there three years.'

'And you haven't married?'

'No! No, I'm not going to marry.'

Amanda shook her head a little sadly. 'I've thought of you often. I know you had a pretty rotten deal as a child. Even before your parents split up, you never really had a home life. I always used to hope that you'd found a man to fall in love with—to love you. I don't like to think of you living alone.'

'I'm used to living alone.' Amanda was so easy to talk to that she found herself confessing, 'Sometimes I think about marriage, mostly because I keep think about having children, but, frankly, the idea of being a mother frightens me. I don't know anything about children.'

'Raising a child is frightening—and tremendously rewarding. You want a man you love beside you, to share the rewards and the troubles.'

'I don't think I have time for marriage—for children. I love teaching, though sometimes——'

Was that a door closing? Someone coming into the hallway? She couldn't hear footsteps. Would a man's step make any sound on that heavy carpet? Her mouth went dry. She focused on Amanda. 'I love it—usually I love it. It's totally absorbing. I get so involved, then sometimes I feel I've lost my energy, that I can't even respond to a student. When I walk into the class, it's always all right, but one morning I might wake up and find myself gone stale. If that happens, I'd have to stop teaching.'

'What would you like to do? Do you have any plans?'

Should she tell Amanda about Jack's job?

'I have a suggestion—something else you could do.' His voice was shockingly smooth and mellow as it broke through their quiet intimacy.

He was leaning casually against the back of a richly overstuffed chair, watching her with a light of mischief in his black eyes, holding her gaze against her will. His dark hair waved deeply over his forehead, softening the strong angles of his face with a hint of boyishness.

He'd always been in trouble, always talking his way out of it with that devilish grin and the gleam in his dark eyes. She had loved him, worshipped him, would have followed anywhere in his footsteps.

Not now. Not any more.

'I didn't expect you to be here.'

Amanda stared, shocked by the flat accusation in Kristy's voice.

'I live here.' He was still smiling, although his eyes grew watchful.

'You live in town. You said——I wouldn't have come if I'd known.'

'You made that plain last night.' His eyes moved slowly over her, down to the curve of her breasts, the narrow waist that flared to feminine hips. When he looked up into her eyes, she knew he was remembering her naked form emerging from the water on Saltspring Island.

He wanted her.

When she was sixteen, she'd have given anything to interest him.

'Is this a plot, then, to deceive me?'

'You know my mother better than that. She doesn't plot. Mother had no reason to think you'd object to my presence.'

'No reason at all,' Amanda was on her feet, a faint flush of anger in her cheeks. 'I'd no idea you two had been fighting. I suppose I should have know, remembering how you—but neither did I expect you here tonight, Blake. You told me you'd be staying in town overnight. Urgent business, you said.'

'Canning cancelled our appointment, so I came home after all. Will dinner stretch to three? Yes? Then I'll have a quick shower and join you ladies in a few minutes.'

He was gone as silently as he had come, leaving Kristy fuming and his mother frowning after him.

'I'm sorry,' Kristy spoke suddenly into the silence. 'I must have been very rude.'

'He probably asked for it. He can be a brat, can't he?'

'Oh, yes! But he's in for a surprise if he thinks I'm about to fall at his feet.'

Kristy couldn't quite make out what Amanda's murmured comment was, but she was grateful when the older woman suggested Kristy help her bring the food out. Dinner could easily have stretched to four or five.

'I've thought of your cooking so often,' Kristy told Amanda as she carried a platter of baked salmon into the dining-room. 'My mouth has been watering all day. You don't have anyone to help you?'

'Not with the cooking. I enjoy that too much. What about you? You used to enjoy cooking.'

'I just throw things together. I've never really had time to learn anything fancy. I do cook a mean pie, though. Remember when you taught me to make pastry?'

'I remember,' Blake's voice intruded, sending shivers down her spine. Thick carpeting should be outlawed around a man like him. She never had any warning. 'You made rhubarb pie for us—too much salt in the pastry.'

'You ate it! And you had seconds.' He held a chair for her. She kept her eyes on the table as she sat down. She wouldn't look at him, wouldn't let him play this game on her.

'I was being a gentleman; I didn't want to hurt your tender feelings. Mother?' He slid out a chair for his mother.

'Not yet, Blake. I'll just bring in the salad. Would you pour us wine? And try to behave yourself.'

'Fat chance,' Kristy muttered.

'Yes, Mother.' He didn't mean a word of that. The devilish grin was lurking there on his face, but his mother was in the next room. She couldn't see it.

'Has anyone ever thrown anything at you, Blake? No, don't pour me any wine. I'm driving.'

'Your next pie was much better,' he conceded, filling her glass despite her protest. 'I couldn't resist finding out if I could still get a rise out of you. Growing up didn't dampen your temper at all, did it?'

'As a matter of fact, it did, but you're——'

'I'm what?'

'What are you up to?'

He sat down across from her, smiling at her even though she was glaring at him. 'What do you think I'm up to?'

'Did you know I'd be at that night-school class? No, you couldn't have.'

He didn't answer.

Kristy said, 'Blake, you never meant to stay away tonight, did you? Last night you told me you wouldn't be here, but——'

'I wanted to see you, but I knew you wouldn't come if I was going to be here. Why is that, Kristy? Why this determination to avoid me? Slipping away from Saltspring Island before the sun is up, foisting me off on that horrifying Delia Devonworth.'

'Delia served you right! You were doing your best to disconcert me in the middle of my class, sneaking up and——'

'Making a play for you,' he suggested.

'But why?'

'Why not? You're a beautiful woman. I went for a lonely walk on the island and there you were. You walked right out of the night and into my arms. That's fate, isn't it? A romantic night. A beautiful redhead. A lonely man.'

'That's not fate. That's a middle-aged chauvinist who's a little bored with life, looking for a new distraction.'

'Putting a label on my may make you feel better, but it won't stop me.'

'You mean you're going to pursue me regardless of my wishes? Don't be an idiot, Blake. I'm not interested.'

'Yes you are. Now hush and pretend to get along with me—for Mother's sake. We can fight later.'

'We'll do nothing later. I'm going home and that's the end of that.'

'Not the end—the beginning,' his low voice promised her as his mother joined them.

'You're crazy!' she hissed.

Kristy had to grin as Blake started updating her on

the doings of mutual friends. This big, aggressive man was determined to have his way, but he was inhibited enough that he had to drop the pursuit while his mother was in the room. His eyes promised her that he would get her later. He would, too. At least, he would try.

'I don't believe it!' Kristy protested when he told her about Linda McKenzie. 'Linda was far too shy. She could never stand up in front of an audience.'

'I'll take you to see her myself. She's performing at a night club in the West End right now. She's still as shy as ever, off stage, but when she stands up there with the band she can really belt out a song.

'I'll have to look her up.'

'How about tomorrow night? I'll take you to dinner, then we'll catch Linda's performance.

'I'm busy tomorrow.' And every night, she told him silently. She flushed as her eyes met his mother's. Amanda wasn't missing any of this, though she came quickly to Kristy's rescue.

'Is your mother planning to use the cottage this summer?'

'No, she's thinking of selling it. She hasn't been out there in years. Do you still go every summer?'

'Usually. Blake takes me out at the beginning of July for a couple of weeks. He has trouble sitting still, so he usually flies back and forth a couple of times to keep up with what's happening at the office.'

'Flies?'

'I lease a seaplane while we're on the island. It's more convenient.'

'I didn't know you were a pilot.'

'There's a lot you don't know about me,' he told her wickedly.

'True. Considering that I haven't seen you in twelve years, we might as well be total strangers.' She turned away from the challenge in his eyes. 'Will you be going back to the island this summer, Amanda?'

'I don't think so. Blake's had all the inactivity he can stand for one summer.'

And Amanda wouldn't go without Blake, mused Kristy. She had always looked after Blake, putting his needs and desires ahead of her own. Obviously, his town apartment was only a sometimes home. He lived here. Did Amanda still cook all his meals? Iron his clothes? What a depressing thought.

'And you, Kristy?' Blake queried softly. 'What about your life outside of work? You don't spend your leisure time on Saltspring Island. You've lived here in Vancouver how long now?'

'Three years.'

'What do you do with your weekends? Your holidays?'

'I live near the beach. Sometimes I go for walks.'

'Alone?'

She could have brought David into this, pulled his name between herself and Blake as a barrier. She wasn't quite sure why she didn't.

'Sometimes. My job keeps me pretty busy. I don't have a lot of time for playing.'

When the telephone rang, Blake went into the next room to answer it. She could hear his voice, low and businesslike.

'It's time I left,' Kristy decided, folding her napkin beside her plate. Dinner was eaten. Her glass of wine and her coffee cup were both empty. If Blake hadn't been here, she would have stayed later. 'I've really enjoyed it.'

'You've spent the whole dinner wanting to throw your plate at my son.'

'I'm sorry.'

'You two always did strike sparks off each other. I used to think your red hair affected Blake like waving red flag at a bull. He's never been able to leave you alone. When you were a child, he used to tease you terribly.'

'I had an awful crush on him back then.'

'I know you did.'

Of course she would have known. The kid next door, always hanging around, always talking about Blake.

'Did he know?'

'I don't think so. He was busy growing up, too, you know. But now——'

'I've loved seeing you again. Could I talk you into coming to dinner at my place? Just you.'

'I'd love to.' She grinned suddenly at Kristy. 'Just me. Blake will have to fight his own battles without my help.'

'There's not going to be any battle.' She wouldn't get herself into this situation again. She'd take care to be sure Blake didn't cross her path. At night school, she'd have Delia so thoroughly wrapped around his neck that he wouldn't be able to move.

'Are you leaving now?'

'Yes. Will you say goodbye to Blake for me?' His voice carried through from the other room, explaining something to the person on the other end. Business.

'Of course.'

'And you'll come to dinner at my place? Next week? Could you come on Tuesday?' Without Blake.

'Tuesday would be lovely. I'd like to see where you're living.'

'I'd like you to see it. It's a nice place. I've got an ocean view from the balcony, and a very nice landlady.' Blake's voice had changed, become brisker. Was he getting ready to end his call? 'I'll go now, before Blake gets off the phone. Otherwise I'll start arguing with him again.'

She almost made it. She was in the car, fitting the

key into the ignition. Then Blake was opening her door, leaning in.

'Don't go yet. I want to talk to you.'

'I don't want to talk to you, Blake. Will you get it through your head that I don't want to see you. I don't want to play games.'

He leaned closer to her. When she was younger, the breadth of his shoulders had made her feel small and feminine in comparison. Not now. She felt threatened by his size, angry at his determined aggressiveness. She could smell the tangy scent of his aftershave. 'Move over,' he instructed in the tones of a man accustomed to getting his way.

'What do you mean, move over?'

'Move over and I'll drive. We'll go somewhere and talk.'

She jerked towards him, her hair flying around her face. 'You're not walking into my life and taking it over, Blake! This is my car! I drive it!' She dragged in a quick, deep breath.

He was watching her, not angry, not exactly amused. Just what was it that glinted in his eyes? 'What on earth is the point of all this? The other night, when we ran into each other on the island, you hadn't seen me in twelve years. Before that, the last time you saw me you couldn't get away fast enough. So what's changed now?'

She'd forgotten how the deep tones of his voice could smile at her, sending shivers along her spine, curving her lips in an answering smile even through her anger. 'Is that why you're so prickly, Kristy? Surely you're not still mad at me twelve years later? That's a bit much, isn't it?'

'I don't want to get involved with you, Blake. Please move—I want to leave.'

'I'm not letting you go.'

'Why? What's the point? There have got to be other

women around who are more willing than I am. If you want an affair, find someone else. Not me!'

He took her hands off the wheel, drew her slowly towards him. She found herself standing outside her car, looking up into dark eyes that were far too close.

'Blake, I want to go home.'

'You have always had the most gorgeous hair, Kristy.' He slipped his hands into it, letting the curls twist around his fingers as he stroked through its length. 'You used to wear it short—wild and curly, like an urchin. I love it long like this, like a cloud of fire.'

'Not like an urchin?'

'No, you're too much of a woman now.' He bent closer, his lips parting slightly as they approached hers.

'No!' She pushed away from him only to find herself backed against her own car, Blake's broad chest between her and the rest of the world. 'Will you let me go!' she demanded, drawing anger around herself as a protection. 'Find someone else to play your games with!'

'But I don't want someone else. I can't think of any other woman who could give me one tenth of the excitement you could.' His voice was low, almost a whisper. 'And it's not an affair I'm after. I've had affairs.' He laughed, a low growl on the night air. 'As you pointed out, Kristy, I'm a middle-aged—er—man.' He was anything but middle-aged. He was handsome and virile and very, very attractive—and he knew it.

'I've sowed my wild oats, Kristy. I'm thirty-five. It's time I settled down, don't you think? And you've walked back into my life at the perfect moment—the girl next door.'

'Just what do you mean by that?' She was unwillingly fascinated. 'What's this role you've cast me in now?'

'A very conventional role, but I think I can promise a certain amount of excitement.' He bent the last fraction of an inch, touching her lips with his own, brushing softly against her mouth.

'No, Blake——'

'Yes,' he insisted, drawing her against him as he slid his hands down from her hair on to her back, taking her mouth with his. 'Yes,' he repeated softly, teasing her lips open with insistent movements of his tongue.

She looked up at him, feeling her body losing its fight, melting into his. Her eyes half closed as his lips firmed on hers. He shifted slightly so that her head rested on his shoulder, his hands moulding her body gently along the length of his.

'I've dreamed of you, Kristy.' His hand caressed her back, her shoulder, threaded through her hair. His fingers spread out through her hair, cupping her head, holding her for his lips and his tongue as he drew the response her lips hadn't wanted to give him. 'You've been haunting me for years.'

'You're twelve years too late, Blake! You should have taken me the night of my sixteenth birthday. I would have done anything for you then. Not any more. The Kristy Murdock who worshipped Blake Harding is so far back she's just a memory. That girl's a stranger to me; it's far too late to call her back.'

'It's obvious that you need some time to get used to the idea, but you may as well accept it. You're going to marry me.'

'You've got to be joking! Marriage is the last thing I'm after. I don't want to marry you—or anyone, for that matter!'

'It's no joke, lady. A year from now, you'll be my wife.' His hand moved suggestively against her hip. 'I'd be surprised if you aren't expecting our first child

by then. So you can stop worrying about your job.
You won't need it.'

'You're crazy, Blake! Maybe you're suffering from
overwork. Maybe you need to see your doctor—or
your psychiatrist!' She had her hands on her hips, her
legs astride in an angry, aggressive stance as she glared
up at him. 'I don't know what's got into you! I don't
want to know! But get this straight! I'm not having
an affair with you! I'm not marrying you! I'm getting
in my car and I'm going home and I'm never going
to see you again!'

'I'll let you go—tonight—but you're certainly going
to see me again. Next Monday, if not sooner. And,
eventually, you'll marry me and have my children.'

'I've got my own life, my own career—a satisfying
life that doesn't require a man to make it worth living.
If I did get married, it certainly wouldn't be to a man
like you! You know exactly what you want, don't
you? What I want or need, even who I really am,
doesn't matter at all.'

'You're gorgeous when you're in a temper.'

'Oh!' She clenched her fists, wanting to throw something at him, to hit out. He wasn't listening to a word
she said. She slammed into her car and managed to
start the engine with a quick, angry burst from the
starter. She rolled down the window and called back
to him as she set the car in motion, 'You want a wife
and kids. I imagine you want someone to cook your
meals and iron your shirts as well! Why don't you put
an ad in the paper?'

Damn him! He was grinning, as if he'd won a
victory. Not at all as if he'd been told off and left
standing alone.

On the way home, as if Blake were watching, her
car shuddered every time she put the clutch in. She
started to tell herself she wasn't about to take the
Honda in for servicing, then realised how childish she

was being. She needed the car to get to her lunch date with her mother, but after that she would drop it off at the garage.

She slipped into Jack's office early the next day. 'I hate to ask, but would you mind if I went early to lunch today? I've a date with my mother over in the West End—I doubt if I can make it in an hour.' Why hadn't she simply insisted on another location for their lunch?'

She knew why. If she'd insisted, her mother wouldn't have been able to spare the time away from her patients.

'You'll leave your students with something to do while you're gone?'

'David is teaching in the next room. He'll keep an eye on them. And they'll have lots to do.'

And they did. Before lunch, she had them started in the designing stages of a lengthy programming assignment. She left Brenda, her most advanced student, in charge of helping any of the others who developed problems in her absence.

It seemed most of Vancouver was rushing to get out of the West End for lunch. Traffic moving into the centre of town wasn't bad at all. Kristy arrived with ten minutes to spare, then spent almost fifteen minutes looking for a parking space. She finally slipped into a small space on Burrard Street just as a Volkswagen vacated. She had to walk four blocks to the professional building, then wait for an lift.

'I'm joining Dr Murdock,' she told the *maître d'hôtel,* following him to the window table where her mother waited with concealed impatience.

'You're late, Kristy. I've already ordered, but Henry will take your order now. I'd recommend the seafood salad.'

Of course she should have ordered the salad, but she knew this kitchen with its elegantly tiny salads. A morning's teaching had left her ravenously hungry.

'Fish and chips? Kristy, you should watch your diet.'

'Why? Am I getting fat?'

Her mother shrugged away this irrelevancy with the ease of a doctor accustomed to ignoring her patients. 'Your body won't forgive this for ever. What a meal! All grease and no fresh vegetables.'

'I eat well enough at home. I think I'll survive the odd meal of fish and chips. How are you, Mother?'

'You should go in for a complete physical. I can put you in touch with a good nutritionist.'

'I really don't think I need it. I feel perfectly healthy.'

'Don't discount what nutritional counselling can do. Dr Galloway is the best in his field. I'll give you a referral—your medical plan will cover the cost.'

'I'll think about it, Mother. Right now I'm pretty busy at work. I may be applying for my boss's job. If I do——'

'Don't ignore your health, Kristy. If you'd seen what I have—the effects of ignoring the needs of your body for too many years. A professional woman must look after herself. After all, you're alone. You've only yourself to rely on. You can't afford to be sick. Not that a married woman is really much better off. So many women live in a fool's paradise, thinking the man will look after everything. If a woman really needs a man, you can be sure he won't be there.'

Next would come the declaration of her father's unworthiness. Verne Murdock had certainly shown himself an uncaring husband and father, but listening to her mother run him down always brought Kristy a futile feeling of depression.

'I really enjoyed my trip out to the island,' she put in, hoping to effect a change of subject. 'I'd almost forgotten how lovely the cottage is.'

'It should sell for a good price, I think. I've arranged for the work that needs doing.'

'That was fast.'

'No point delaying. The cottage is useless to me.'

'Until it's sold, would you mind if I went out there for the odd weekend?'

'I don't care. Just be sure you don't leave a mess—after all, I am trying to sell. And don't get in the way of the workmen. But I didn't want to talk to you about the island.' Stephanie waved that away with an economical gesture of her hand. In between words she was efficiently despatching her salad. The eating hardly interfered with her talking.

'What did you walk to talk about?' The fish and chips that Henry placed in front of her looked delicious—big chunks of steaming home-made potato chips nestled around succulent pieces of fish in batter fried to a golden beauty.

'Computers.'

'Computers?'

Her mother frowned repressively. 'Kristy, I don't think you'll make a positive impression on your students if you talk to them with that blank tone. Computers. It is your specialty, isn't it?'

'I work with them. You know that.'

'You did consultations in Toronto, didn't you? And you did your master's thesis on small business data-base systems.'

'Yes. That's what I'm working on still—teaching people the basics of——'

'Well, I imagine you must know something about it. I haven't time to go into it myself. I have hospital rounds in a few minutes. Will you phone up my office manager and make an appointment to see her? I want you to set up a system for my office. We've got such an assortment of odds and ends that it's rapidly turning into chaos.'

'Mother, that's a big job. Your information needs are pretty complex. I can't just set up a system over lunch.'

'I'm aware of that. Miss Devonworth, my office manager, will make herself available to you at weekends. I'm sure you'll find her co-operative. You've not finished those chips yet? I'll have to go, Kristy. You will make the phone call?'

'Devonworth?' Delia Devonworth? 'I'll make it,' she agreed, then ate her meal in solitude, wondering why she couldn't have told her mother a simple no.

How many weekends would she lose doing a job that a consultant would charge thousands of dollars for? If it had been a personal service for her mother, something Stephanie needed, she honestly thought she wouldn't begrudge the time. But this was a mere convenience, because her mother couldn't be bothered selecting and instructing a consultant.

Kristy knew why she hadn't said no. She hadn't wanted to watch her mother's eyes turn cold and distant.

She paid for her lunch—Stephanie had had their bills made out separately—and returned to the street. After running through a sudden summer shower, she arrived at her car only to find a parking ticket on her windscreen.

CHAPTER FOUR

DAVID accepted her decision to cancel their date philosophically. 'Next Wednesday, then,' he suggested. No wonder she found him so easy to be with. He accepted her devotion to her work, seldom complained when she had to cancel a date.

Not that this was anything to do with her work at the college. She couldn't even describe it as a family obligation. She had a feeling she was being a fool, spending most evenings working in her mother's office with Delia—the same tense, not-very-bright Delia Devonworth who had appeared in Kristy's night-school class on Monday. Delia certainly wasn't enjoying the process, and Kristy wasn't even sure that her mother would be particularly grateful for her efforts.

Saturday and Sunday she spent with Delia, finally arriving at a point where she could assign Delia a task of collecting information, leaving Kristy free of this crazy job for a few days.

She overslept on Monday morning, the accumulation of too many late nights and no days off. She had a whole week to get through before she could sleep in. Night school tonight, then tomorrow she was having Amanda for dinner. Regretfully, she phoned Amanda and put the dinner off for a week.

'I'm sorry, but I've been doing this job for my mother and I'm just beat.'

'Don't worry about it, Kristy. Get a good rest. I'll be looking forward to next week. If there's anything I can do, be sure to call me.'

Jack called her into his office on Monday morning.

'You look terrible,' he informed her impersonally. 'Don't tell me one night-school class has done this to you?'

'No. My mother has. I'm doing a job for her, reorganising her data system. It's turned into a pretty big job.'

'And how's the night-school class going?'

'Pretty well. They're a good bunch, very sharp and eager to absorb all the newest. You didn't have someone else that could take it over, did you?'

'Not a chance. I'm working on an instructor for the next time, but you're stuck with this one. Incidentally, you've been short-listed for the director's job along with Kinney and two outsiders. The interviews will be held the end of the week.'

'Jonathan Kinney's being interviewed?'

'That's not significant. Any staff member who applies automatically gets an interview. You don't have to worry about him.'

Kristy wasn't so sure. In the last few days she'd frequently seen Kinney talking earnestly with either Dr McAllister or the bursar. She suspected he was playing politics, using whatever influence he had to try to assure himself of the job.

'Who will be on the interview board, Jack? Or can't you tell me that?'

'I'll be there, as well as Dr McAllister. The third member hasn't been selected yet. It's Dr McAllister you have to worry about. Be prepared for him to try to throw in a trick question—Would you quit if you got married? What would you do it you decided to have a child? What if your husband got a transfer?'

'I'm not married. None of that applies.'

'That won't stop Mac. Just try to be ready. Don't let him ruffle you.'

'I'll play it like a politician. Whatever he asks, I'll

tell him what I want to talk about. "Miss Murdock, do you have any plans to marry?" Well, Dr McAllister, I've been here for three years. I think I'm familiar with the workings of the department and——'

'Don't try it. The man has no sense of humour.'

There was no point worrying about it. She'd go to the interview as well prepared as she could. She'd answer questions as honestly and completely as she could. The rest was out of her hands.

By the time Darren came to her place that evening, Kristy had forgotten about the interview. At the end of a long, very trying day, it was all she could do to get herself to the night class. She let Darren carry out an armful of marking for her and they drove to the college, Kristy silent at the wheel while Darren talked about Marion and her excitement over the coming baby.

Blake was early, waiting in the hallway with the insurance man and his wife. She opened the lab door and Darren set her papers down on the desk. When she went to the storeroom door, Blake was suddenly at her side, taking the keys out of her hand.

'I can open that door without any help!' she protested as he fitted the key into the lock. 'I do it every day.'

'Shh,' he warned softly. 'What will your students think if they hear you talking like this?'

'They'll think you're giving me a hard time!'

'Am I? Have you got used to the idea yet?'

'What idea?'

'Being my wife. I took you by surprise the other day, didn't I?'

'Surprise is hardly the word for it. I think you're insane. You may as well propose to a stranger.'

His eyes dropped to trace the curves of her body under her dress. 'Strangers?' His finger traced along the side of her neck, down towards the white skin that was exposed just below the neck. 'I don't——'

'Stop it! Behave yourself! Now, will you please get out of here!' She opened a cupboard and slammed some manuals down on to the shelf.

'Do you want these ones taken to the lab?'

'I don't need help!'

'You asked Darren to help you last week. It's my turn this week.'

'Are you going to spend the whole evening harassing me?'

He grinned. 'That's an idea. Maybe I could black-mail you. If you don't marry me and have my child, I'll get up in front of your class and tell them what a hellion you were. I'll tell them——'

'I don't doubt you would. I can see you with that wicked gleam in your eye, being an absolute bas—'

'Now, now, Kristy. That's not ladylike at all.'

'Some day you're going to be murdered in your bed, Blake Harding.'

'By you? In bed? It might almost be worth it.'

She couldn't help laughing. 'You're impossible, Blake! I don't believe this is happening. I've got a class to teach. Will you please stop being a brat and smarten up!'

'On one condition. Come out with me for a coffee afterwards. If I'm going to put up with Delia for another night, I deserve some reward, Do you realise that woman phoned me three times last week, asking for advice, suggesting we meet to work together?'

'You could safely have accepted her offer. She's been too busy to meet anyone this week. She's my mother's office manager. Delia and I have been together almost every evening, working on a new information system for Mother's office.'

'Then you're the one who deserves a reward. That woman's a—I can't describe her adequately and main-tain my reputation as a gentleman. Don't snort, Kristy.

It isn't ladylike. I tell you what. I'll keep Delia out of your hair tonight, then afterwards we'll——'

'I can't. I'm driving Darren home.'

'He can come, too. He'll be our chaperon. Why are you working nights for your mother?'

She shrugged. 'Just a favour. Darren will want to get home. His wife——'

'We'll drop him off first.'

'I'm not going out alone with you, Blake.'

'What are you afraid of?'

'You. Are you going to behave yourself tonight? I can't teach a class if you're going to——'

'I'll be good. Scout's honour.'

'I didn't know you were a Scout.'

He laughed. 'I wasn't.'

He did behave. He even helped Delia without complaint.

Kristy always tried to get her students involved, contributing to the learning process. Surprisingly, Blake was an ideal class member. He had exciting ideas about applications for the programs they were working with, things she had never thought of. But he was also willing to absorb other people's ideas with enthusiasm.

Watching the project he was developing on the computer, Kristy decided that Blake was probably very successful at his job. He was so incredibly quick to grasp new ideas and apply them. The model he was developing was beautiful in its intricate efficiency, although totally bewildering to Delia who had watched him build it.

He wasn't so absorbed in his project that he forgot to watch Kristy. Several times during the evening, she straightened up from helping someone, only to find Blake's eyes on her, dark and intense.

When the class ended, he was at her side, picking up a pile of manuals and carrying them into the storeroom. She accepted his help silently. When she locked the storeroom door, he stood watching her, then followed her to the staffroom.

'I can get my coat by myself, you know.'

'Can you?' He slipped it off the hanger and held it out for her.

'I don't need help getting dressed, or buttoning up.' But he had turned her round and was buttoning up the coat, his eyes on his fingers as if he had to concentrate on what he was doing.

'There, all buttoned up. Did you get your car into the garage this week?'

'Yes. Not because you told me to, but——'

He laughed. 'You're a contrary girl, aren't you? Were you going to try to run away on me again tonight? We're going for coffee, remember.'

'Darren——'

'I already talked to Darren. You were right. He does want to go home to his Marion. Apparently he's in a permanent state of wedded bliss—you should try it yourself some time. Now, now, don't start shooting sparks again. Young Darren would like us to come to his place for coffee. Marion, it seems, would love to see you again.'

'I don't want to——'

'See Marion? Why not?'

'Of course I want to see Marion. But they're sure to misunderstand. If I go there with you, they're sure to wonder what's between us. There's nothing between us and I don't want everyone getting the wrong idea.'

'Too late now, my dear. I've already accepted on your behalf.'

'I've been wondering why you hadn't married, but I think I'm beginning to understand it. No girl would be willing to put up with having her life managed like this. All right, I'll come, but keep your hand off my elbow, and don't you dare reach for my keys. You're not driving my car.'

Darren was waiting in the hallway, smiling. 'I just called Marion. She'll have the coffee ready for us. She'll be thrilled to see you again.

Marion and Darren had made the small suite into a comfortable home for themselves. Kristy let Marion push her into a comfortable bean bag chair; Blake ended up in a similar chair, his long legs sticking up awkwardly.

'You'll never get out of that chair,' Kristy said when Darren and Marion disappeared into the kitchen.

'Don't fool yourself. Just try running and I'll show you how quickly I can move.'

'I'm not running. More to the point, I'm not in the running. That's the only reason I agreed to have coffee with you tonight, to make it clear that——'

'Coffee here,' announced Darren. He was carrying the tray. Behind him, an obviously pregnant Marion held the cream and sugar bowls.

'Cream and sugar, Ms Murdock?'

'Kristy,' she corrected. 'Just cream, thanks. You're looking really good, Marion.' It was true. She was glowingly happy, her youthful face rounded softly by her pregnancy.

'I feel great, too. Big, and awkward,' she patted the roundness under her smock, 'but I'm looking forward so much to the baby.'

'Are you going to keep on working?'

'I don't think so. I haven't decided really, but I think I'll quit working. Darren has to work overtime so often, it would be hard to do a good job of parenting with both of us working.'

Darren sat down beside his wife. 'We've got a lot happening at work. I'll be snowed under until the new store has been open and running for a while. Until then, I'm not going to be much help to Marion with the baby.'

They smiled fondly at each other. Kristy looked away, and found herself staring into Blake's black eyes.

Darren said, 'This apartment is too small, but David's been talking about moving, buying a house. If he does, we can move into his suite—it's bigger, just about perfect for us.'

Later, as they left Darren and Marion, Blake caught her arm and asked, 'Who's David?'

'He teaches at the college.'

'That's not what I mean. Who is he to you?'

He was too perceptive. She shook his hand off. 'What business is that of yours?' She got into the front seat of her car. 'You can walk from here, can't you? If not, there's a bus at the next corner.'

'You didn't tell me there was anyone else.'

She stared at the steering wheel, answering without looking at Blake. 'David and I go out a couple of times a week. We're friends—more than friends. He's asked me to marry him.'

'You said you weren't engaged. You told me——'

'I'm not. I don't want to be. I don't want to marry David and I don't want to marry you. I'm happy with my life the way it is—my job, my friends. Why should I go looking for unhappiness?'

The night sounds of the city washed over them as Blake stared down at her. 'Is he your lover?'

'Yes.' She took a deep breath, then said, 'Blake, I want you to leave me alone. We were friends once, but after what happened at—when——'

'You mean, after we made love on your sixteenth birthday?'

'Yes——No, we didn't. Not—I don't want any kind of involvement with you, Blake. Not any more. To be honest, it—it terrifies me.' She started the engine

quickly, driving away without looking at him, trying
to pretend he wasn't even there.

The next day she worked on putting Blake out of
her mind. Events helped. She was busy at work. She
spent her lunch hour rushing some papers to Delia.
When she came out of her mother's office, she found
her car adorned with another summons from the City
of Vancouver.

'Because,' as she explained to David later, 'I forgot
to feed money to the darned parking meter when I
parked.'

By then she was getting over the tensions of the
day, relaxing in front of the fire she'd lit to chase
away the dampness from the rain outside. She had lit
the fire when she arrived home from work, knowing
David was coming and would appreciate the warmth.
Then she'd spent twenty minutes relaxing in a hot
bath before slipping into a long, flowing caftan.

She recognised David's light tap on the door and
called to him to let himself in.

'I'm too lazy to get up.' She was curled up, half
sitting against a pile of soft cushions on the carpet in
front of the fire, a drink of lemonade in her hand.
'There's a jug of lemonade in the fridge. Help yourself.
Or if you want something stronger——'

'I know where it is. Don't get up.'

Nothing could have induced her to get up. Twenty
minutes more in front of the fire and she might begin
to regain some of her vitality, but not yet. She stared
at the fire while she waited for David to join her,
formless thoughts in her mind.

David came back with a glass in his hand. He found
himself a cushion and joined her on the carpet.

'I didn't start anything for dinner. I thought maybe
a pizza?' She watched him loosen the tie that helped
give him a businesslike image at the college. With his
boyishly curly blond hair, David had to dress delib-

erately to distinguish himself from the students.

'Sounds find. Shall I order it?'

It was one of the things she liked about him. Not only did he like pepperoni pizza, but he was perfectly willing to accept that she was too tired after a day's work to worry about cooking or hostessing.

'And how was your mother?' David had never met her mother, but he always remembered to ask after her.

'I didn't see her. Just Delia, her office manager.'

The pizza came. David opened the cardboard box while Kristy put another piece of wood on the fire and plugged some moody music into the stereo. David cleared away when the eating was done.

'That's the way I like to do dishes,' he told her. 'Just throw it into the garbage.' He rearranged the cushions and she curled up against him, her head on his shoulder.

'I'm taking the girls to the maritime museum this weekend,' he told her in one of the spaces between the music. 'You could come along.'

She had avoided meeting his daughters. Children of a broken marriage, grabbing a few moments with their father. She remembered how badly she had needed her father, how many times she had made an uncomfortable third, intruding on her father and his latest woman.

One of the troubles with marriage was handling the break-up. David was luckier than some other people she knew; his divorce seemed to have been reasonably amicable. It hadn't stopped him from thinking of marriage again.

The music quickened, losing its slow moodiness. David's hand slid along the silky fabric of her caftan. When she turned her head, his lips took hers with a gentle possessiveness. The music had stirred her blood and her body, drawing a response from her like passion.

Then her eyes opened and the dark man in her mind dissolved into the youthful charm of David.

She was relieved when the doorbell rang. Her kiss had been like a promise, making it difficult to plead tiredness or a headache.

It would be Paula, forgetting that Wednesday was David's night. Kristy would invite her in, offer coffee. Paula was astute enough to take the hint and stick around until David left.

If Paula hadn't come, Kristy would have had to send him away in any case. The music and the fire had conspired to call up Blake's ghost to haunt her. She daren't close her eyes for fear her lover would be replaced by Blake's dark threat.

'Ignore it,' murmured David when the doorbell rang again before Kristy had herself untangled from his arms.

'It'll be Paula, and she knows I'm here. My car's outside.'

'If you don't answer, she'll have the sense to go away.'

She walked across the carpet in her bare feet, feeling the coolness as she stepped off the carpet.

'Come on in,' she was saying as she opened the door, before she saw him.

He was smiling that smile, stepping towards her even as she started to close the door again.

'You did invite me in.'

'No. Not you.' His arm was resting against the door, preventing her from closing it. 'Please leave, Blake. I have company and I don't——'

'Surely you can introduce me to your friends.' His eyes had narrowed, taking in the fullness of her lips, the disarray of her hair, her bare feet. 'You may as well let me in. I'm not going away until you do.'

'This is my home. You have no right——'

'Let me in, Kristy.' He grasped her shoulders with his hands and moved her firmly aside.

'Stop manhandling me! Get out!'

He ignored her, pushed past her and walked into the living-room. He was taking in every detail with black eyes that glittered dangerously—the fire, the pile of soft cushions that supported David, David himself with his tie gone, his shirt half unbuttoned.

David spluttered, 'I don't know who you are, but I think you'd better——'

'Blake Harding.'

Kristy watched Blake approaching David. She was frozen, knowing he was going to do something, knowing she couldn't stop him.

He stopped two steps away from David. He was smiling.

'This is David Roswell.' She glared at Blake. 'Blake isn't staying,' she told David. 'He's just leaving.'

'I'm not in that much of a hurry, Kristy.' If she hadn't seen his eyes, she could almost have believed he was as nonchalant as he sounded. 'I like the sound of your music. Perhaps I'll just stay to listen for a bit.'

'You will not! I don't want you here, Blake!'

'I think you'd better leave, Harding.' David was standing behind her, working hard at sounding threatening. He wasn't good at it.

Blake laughed.

'Look here,' David began angrily, 'whoever you are—'

'Get out, Blake!' Kristy demanded, knowing David's anger would only make Blake worse.

He didn't seem to hear her. 'David Roswell,' he speculated, his eyes dismissing this rival, moving to Kristy as if he were taking possession of her. He did it deliberately, not hiding the journey of his gaze—from her tousled hair, down to the modest opening of her caftan at her neck; further, to the curve of her breasts beneath the fabric.

Anyone watching them would believe that Blake's eyes told a story of possession. As if they had been lovers. As if he had only to reach out a hand to make her his.

'I think, Roswell, that it makes more sense if you're the one to leave, not me.'

'Blake, you have got one hell of a nerve! So help me, if you don't get out of here, I'm calling the police! I'll charge you with breaking and entering. I'll——'

'Darling, once you get over being angry, you won't do any of that, and you know it. Now tell your friend to run along. You and I have things to say to each other—alone.'

'Kristy, just who is this man? What is he to you? He talks as if——Are you and him—I mean, you and he——'

'Is that all it takes for you to start accusing me of things—for a stranger to walk in and start making suggestive comments?'

'He doesn't sound like a stranger. You don't talk to him as if he were a stranger.'

'Damnit, David! Why do you turn to me, questioning me, when this—this damned macho male comes breaking into my apartment uninvited? You've known me long enough to know I'm not——'

'You don't know her at all.' Blake's voice was light, deceptively friendly. 'And whatever relationship you've had, it's over now. I'm here and you're finished, David. I suggest you find your tie and get out.'

Kristy found herself screaming at Blake, not even knowing what the words were. 'You pig! You damned chauvinist pig! You think wanting something means you've got possession? That's all that matters, isn't it? What you want! Well, I don't want you! Now get out of here, or so help me——'

David was grumbling, 'Kristy, I think you should have told me. After all——'

'You, too!' She turned on him. 'Both of you, get out!' She grasped David's shoulder and pushed him against Blake, pushed them both in the direction of the door without touching Blake directly. 'Both of you get out and don't come back! I'm sick of both of you!'

David was going; he was already moving towards the door. Blake wasn't. She knew there was no way she could get him out of the door. He was too big, too strong, and, no matter how loud she screamed, he wasn't moving an inch. If he stayed, if she ended this evening alone with him, with David gone——

She fell silent abruptly. David wasn't even looking back. Blake was watching her, arms crossed. The shouting wasn't affecting him at all. Paula or Dean would be up any minute, or sending the police to break up the disturbance. Paula would be shocked to hear Kristy screaming insults at Blake. It wasn't like the Kristy she knew.

Bringing the police wouldn't help anything at all. Blake would be here, greeting them, totally in control. Kristy would be hysterical, sounding like a fool.

She could walk out behind David, go downstairs and seek refuge with Paula and Dean. She would feel a fool, but it would get her away from Blake.

The bell of the telephone rang stridently into the silence. 'Will you please leave?' she asked, her voice low and husky.

'Now that he's gone,' Blake agreed, watching her. 'I've certainly made you angry, haven't I? It couldn't be helped—I wasn't leaving him here alone with you.' He glanced thoughtfully at the door where David had disappeared only seconds ago. 'I doubt that he'll be back.' His smile was totally without humour. 'Don't you think you should answer the phone? It's going to keep ringing until you do.'

'Are you all right?' demanded Paula loudly as Kristy picked up the receiver.

'It's my landlady,' she told Blake drily. Their eyes met in a long silence she could not put words to.

'Do you want me to call the police?' demanded Paula's voice in her ear.

'Are you leaving?' she asked Blake.

'Yes, dear, I am leaving.' He stepped closer. She should have been telling Paula to call the police, or get upstairs herself, but she stood frozen as Blake touched her hair, smoothing the wild curls with a hand that was suddenly incredibly gentle.

'Kristy? Are you all right? If you don't answer, I'm calling the police right now! Then I'm going to——'

'No. It's OK.'

It was anything but OK. Blake's lips came closer, brushing hers, hardly touching, a feathery caress that moved from her mouth to her cheek. She pressed her lips together, hard, to stop the trembling, to shut him out.

'I'll be back,' he promised her, his mouth a sudden, hard pressure on hers before he stepped away.

'Are you sure? Are you OK?' Paula's voice demanded loudly in her ear.

'Tell her to call off the cavalry,' Blake instructed wryly. 'I'll see you tomorrow.'

'No, you won't. Not tomorrow, not——'

'Want to bet?' he taunted her softly.

'I'm not a child. You can't catch me with a dare or a bet.'

'I'm coming up!' Paula announced loudly in her ear.

'It'll take more than dares and bets,' agreed Blake, 'but in the end——'

'Never!' She was still holding the telephone receiver,

the dialling tone wailing in her ear. Suddenly it all seemed so ridiculous. 'You're crazy! This whole scene is insane. That's my landlady pounding at the door. God knows what she thinks of all this.'

The door burst open with a crash.

'Kristy, what on earth? Are you OK? Who is this man?'

Kristy shrugged helplessly, unable to find words to describe Blake.

'I'm leaving,' Blake assured Paula with a smile. 'Kristy's not up to introducing me, so I'll do it myself. I'm Blake Harding. You can expect to see quite a bit of me.'

'You're——' Paula was shaking her head, bewildered both by Kristy's silence and Blake's calm assurance.

'Blake. The man who's marrying Kristy.'

CHAPTER FIVE

'Who——' Paula took a quick check around the room, looking for signs of violence. 'I saw David drive up—after all, it is Wednesday. Then, later, footsteps going up your stairs. I was just tucking Denny into bed. Then the shouting started.'

'I'm sorry about Denny's bedtime. Tell him——'

'Oh, he's off to sleep by now. I lent him my Walkman, plugged him into some loud music. He went off to sleep thinking he was in seventh heaven. Dean's out, working at the UBC library on his thesis. Otherwise, I'd have sent him up to borrow some sugar or something, just in case you wanted rescuing.'

Kristy found she could move. She got to the easy chair and sank down shakily.

'The way you were going on, I came tearing up here, thinking he might be violent.'

'There was a moment when I thought he was going to hit David. But I have a feeling I was the violent one—doing all the screaming.'

Paula picked up a cushion from the floor and plumped it into the corner of the sofa before sitting down herself. 'You certainly were. I was quite impressed. I wouldn't have had the nerve to scream at him—I somehow doubt if anyone's ever done it before.'

'I've done it before, but not since I was sixteen.'

'An old lover?'

'He's never been my lover.'

'Well, don't you think it might be a good idea? I mean, before you actually go to the extent of marrying this fellow. The good-looking ones aren't always the best lovers. You never know——But, Kristy, what about David? If you're marrying this man, what about David?'

Kristy felt a choking that was almost laughter in her throat. Blake would pass any test as a lover. She remembered his hands on her, his mouth against her skin. His touch was too good, his kiss too easy to remember. She dragged her fingers through her hair, pushing hard against her scalp to dim the headache that was growing.

'I am not, repeat, not, marrying Blake Harding. No matter what he says. And as for David—David couldn't get out of here fast enough tonight. He thinks there may be something between Blake and me, so you might not be seeing too much of David after this. Well, that's not a tragedy. It wasn't going to last much longer in any case. I've applied for his boss's job.'

She locked the door when Paula left.

With the curtains pulled and the stereo off, her apartment was deathly silent. Kristy padded across the floor in bare feet, slipping out of her caftan and under the covers of her big antique bed.

She picked up the book she'd been reading over the last week. The story had started out as a real gripper, but tonight she couldn't get up any interest for it.

She couldn't remember Blake ever failing to get what he wanted before. But she wasn't his kind of woman. If she were, then her father might have been able to love her. They were two of a kind, Blake and her father. They both wanted their women soft and agreeable, content to devote everything to making their men comfortable. Kristy wasn't that kind of woman, any more than her mother had been.

Kristy pushed her pillow into shape, twisting, curling herself into a huddle beneath the blankets.

Damn Blake, bursting into her life with his fantasies.

The telephone rang into the silence of her night. She wouldn't answer. Eventually, he would give up. The ringing seemed to go on forever, but she knew it must stop.

She heard a stirring below. Was the noise disturbing Denny's sleep?

She stumbled out of bed. She was tangled somehow in the blankets. She pulled impatiently, freed herself and hurried towards the living-room.

The ringing seemed louder now. She could feel Blake, as if he were at her side, urging her to answer. She remembered their meeting on Saltspring Island, how the darkness had drawn her into his arms.

She watched her hand lifting the receiver.

'Kristy?'

Once, he had taken her climbing on a cliff far on the other side of the island. She'd followed him, climbing rocks at his heels until the moment she had suddenly looked down.

She'd had no idea how far they had come. From below, the cliff had looked an easy climb.

She had felt the roughness of the rocks beneath her fingers as she gripped convulsively with her hands. Some of the shale crumbled into her fingers. She had had a terrifying, hypnotic vision of the rock breaking away beneath her hands and feet, throwing her to her death on the jagged ground below.

'Kristy?' The question, quiet, demanding her attention, calling her to follow him. He had drawn her eyes to his. Quietly, he had given her instructions, guided her hands and feet with his words.

As long as she kept her eyes on Blake, his voice in her ears, she could do anything, climb any mountain.

'Are you all right, Kristy?'

She didn't want to talk to him tonight. She set the receiver carefully into its cradle.

He would call back. She watched the telephone as

if it were Blake himself. She knew, felt the ringing the instant before it started again.

It stopped when she pulled the plug from the wall.

He wouldn't give up.

In the morning she could apply for a new number. An unlisted number.

Tonight, knowing the phone would ring if she plugged it back in, she couldn't sleep in this apartment. She put on her jeans and a warm sweater. The rain had stopped, but it was a cool night.

Outside, the air smelled freshly washed. There was only a faint wind blowing, but she could hear the slow surf as she walked towards the grassy park that bordered the beach.

When morning came, the beach would slowly fill with Vancouver's children on summer holidays—children ranging from a week to ninety years old. The young girls would spread themselves over the beach, exposing their smooth skin to the sun, pretending not to notice the eyes of the boys and men who walked past.

Children and sandcastles, mothers counting heads.

Tonight she had the beach to herself. She slipped her shoes off and walked until she came to a big log embedded in the sand. Sitting with the log against her back, she could look out across English Bay.

No wonder it held such fascination for photographers—the city lights reaching for the sky, reflected in the water, streaking across the bay.

On Saltspring Island, on the night of her sixteenth birthday, only the few cabin lights had reflected across the water.

Her birthday party had been a mixture. Her parents had come to make a rare appearance at the island, inviting the more prestigious of the neighbours to dinner and dancing.

Then there had been Kristy's friends, ranging from

teenagers to young adults. For Kristy, it had been more than a birthday party . . .

This was goodbye. Tomorrow, she would leave with her father, would catch the jet from Vancouver to Toronto. She would probably never see this cottage —or Blake—again. With youthful single-mindedness, she knew that he was the only boy she could ever love. She knew that Blake had never even thought of her in that way; he thought of her as a child. Jealously, she had watched the spark flaring in his eyes for other, older girls.

Some day he would look at her that way.

Her party dress was as daring as their current housekeeper would let her get away with. The bodice hugged the new maturity of her breasts, showing a soft, unmistakably womanly swelling above the low-cut gown. The skirt swirled from her waist in a froth of feminine lace.

For a moment, when she greeted Blake at the door, she thought his eyes flashed, seeing her as the woman she was.

Wishful thinking, because he quickly annexed Sheila Cunningham's attention, holding her in his arms through dance after dance.

They were standing together, Blake and Sheila, when the slow waltz started. Kristy's heart was pounding in her ears, but she forced herself to approach them, swallowing to clear her throat so she could ask,

'Will you dance with me, Blake?'

He hesitated, glancing at Sheila.

Sheila shrugged. 'Go ahead. Dance with the kid.'

He held her stiffly, awkwardly, as they moved away from Sheila.

'I'm leaving in the morning,' she told him flatly,

staring over her shoulder at her mother and father standing together, a world separating them. Picture of a successful marriage. They were greeting guests, no sign of strife between them, no indication that tomorrow Verne would fly to Toronto with Kristy, leaving Stephanie behind.

'You should have a good flight. The weather's been clear all across the country.'

'Will you take me outside, Blake? I want to look at the lights on the water.'

'It's cool. You'd be too cold in that dress.'

'Please, Blake!'

She slipped out of his arms, catching his hand and tugging, urging him to come with her. 'It's my last night.'

He humoured her, letting her pull him away from the party.

Outside, they walked hand in hand, silently moving through the shadows as they strolled down the long hillside towards the water.

There wasn't another soul in the entire world, only Blake and Kristy under a moonlit sky.

At the bottom of the lawn they were concealed by the trees. When Kristy looked back, she couldn't see the house at all, only the lights stretching out over the upper part of the lawn.

He couldn't see her. The darkness was so deep here. He stopped walking when she did. She could sense his eyes above her, looking out over the water.

'Kiss me, Blake,' she whispered in the darkness.

'What?'

'Please, Blake! Just once. Kiss me the way you were kissing Sheila last week. I saw you, on your porch.'

'Kristy! You don't know what you're talking about. Sheila's a woman; you're——'

'I'm not a child, Blake. Not any more. Please. Just once.' She came close to him, touching his shoulders with her hands, tentatively, wanting to touch, yet afraid. 'I'm leaving tomorrow,' she whispered.

He was so silent, staring down at her in the dark. In a moment he would step away, shake her touch off and leave her alone in the night.

She would always be alone. Already, she had realised that her father was not completely happy about her coming with him to Toronto. She was his girl, but only when he wanted her near.

Before Blake could step away, she reached her arms around his neck, pulling her young body against his, her lips to his. She gave him the soft, innocent kiss of her youth, her lips closed. His hands came up to her shoulders, gripping her to push her away.

'Love me, Blake. Please! Just for a few minutes. I just want you to kiss me. Just once! You can go back to Sheila after, but——'

His lips crushed hers into silence. His hands caressed the bare skin of her back, moulding her body against the unexpectedly hard maleness of his.

Her mouth opened on a gasp as he pressed hard against her. His tongue slipped through, taking her mouth with a man's passion that left her spinning.

She hardly knew when he lowered her to the grass, only felt the coolness of damp grass against her back as he slipped the zipper down along her back.

His mouth was on her lips, her face, her eyes. When her head fell back against his arm, his mouth took her neck as his hands caressed her bare shoulders and her back, searching for the fastening of her strapless brassière.

She was hardly aware of his man's needs, knew only that she was held tightly in his arms at last. She wasn't even conscious of the noise that escaped her throat as the cold air rushed against her suddenly freed breasts.

He drew back, left her lying on the grass with her

bodice around her waist, the cold air on her naked skin and Blake's dark form over her.

'Kristy, we mustn't. I'm——'

'Don't go,' she begged, pressing her lips against his in the contact that had turned his body hard against her only moments ago. She slipped her arms up around his neck, tangling her fingers in his hair, pulling him towards her.

He held himself stiffly away from her, rigid as she pulled his head down, pressing her lips against his, moving her tongue in a daring imitation of his earlier kiss.

He groaned her name, taking charge of the kiss, pulling her softness against his hardness. He pushed her back down on to the grass, his lips devouring hers, his tongue taking her mouth in a hard passion.

His hands moulded her breasts, caressing the nipples to a sensitive rigidity that left her trembling in his arms, incoherently begging him not to stop.

When his mouth covered the sensitive peak of one breast, she thought she would die from the feelings stirring inside her. She didn't realise she had cried out until he responded with a more urgent passion.

His hands roamed over her hips, her thighs, pushing the lacy fabric aside, sending her spinning dizzily away from reality. Somehow his own shirt was open and her hands were exploring the strange feel of hair on his chest.

Spinning, dizzy——The touch of his hand between her legs was a sudden shock. She gasped, tensing, suddenly frightened, staring at his dark head as it blocked the sky from her sight.

'Blake?' Her uncertainty, her innocence, quivered in her voice.

His hands left her with a rough suddenness. 'You'd better go back. Get dressed and go back.'

'Don't go, Blake. Kiss me again.'

'You don't know what you're saying, Kristy. Get yourself dressed and get back to the house where you belong.'

'I do know, Blake. I'm not a kid. If you want to——If you want to do it, Blake, I'll let you.' Her hands dropped away from their protective covering of her naked breasts in a gesture of surrender that he couldn't see.

He cursed angrily in the darkness. His hand grasped her arm roughly, pulling her to her feet. 'Will you get to hell out of here? You're crazy, Kristy! You have no idea. You're surely not on the pill, and I don't have——I can just see it—you sixteen and pregnant, and——'

Her trembling fingers struggled with the bra. Even in the dark, she felt a little less vulnerable once she had her dress around her again.

'We could get married. If I got pregnant, we could get married. I'd like to have your baby, Blake. I promise you, I'd be a good wife. We could——'

'No, we couldn't. Now get to hell away from me, Kristy. I don't want you in my arms and I certainly don't want to marry you.' His hand grasped her arm, pushed her roughly in the direction of the house. 'Go! Get up to that house. It's way past your bedtime.'

And now, twelve years later, it was still way past her bedtime.

Kristy lifted her wrist and pushed the button to light her watch. Three o'clock. In a few hours she should be getting up, having breakfast, planning her day at work. If she dashed home to bed, fell asleep immediately, she might manage almost four hours' sleep.

On the other hand, she could have a bath and drive out for an early breakfast somewhere, then go to work early. Alone, with no interruptions, she could usually get through a tremendous amount of work at the college.

She made her way home and ran her bath, hoping the noise wouldn't disturb anyone below. She had caused the Barnays enough disturbance tonight. Then she slipped quietly out of the old house and drove to an all-night restaurant for an early breakfast.

The streets were empty except for an occasional solitary pedestrian. The driver of a police patrol car gave her a sharp look as she drove past. Later, on her way to the college, she passed a group of students, walking hand in hand, singing loudly into the early morning air. One of them shouted a greeting. She wound down her window and called back to them.

As she had hoped, the college was deserted. Even the janitors had gone. She let herself in, made a pot of coffee in the staffroom, and set to work in her office. Seemingly hours later, she looked up from her marking to find Jack standing at her office door.

'Been at it all night?'

'Just since around six. I think I'm caught up now.'

'About your interview. I told you it's Friday afternoon? Yes, well, the board is going to be made up of me, McAllister, and someone from the advisory board.'

'Who?'

He shrugged. 'Whoever they select. Speaking of the board, what the hell is UNIX, Kristy?'

'An operating system for computers. It supports networking, but it's more sophisticated than the networking system we're using.'

'There you are. I knew you'd be on top of it. We've been getting suggestions from the board lately about UNIX.'

When the library opened at eight she was on the phone to Tom, the librarian.

'UNIX? Hold on while I key it in. No, no books.

These computer things are impossible, you know.
Everything changes so fast. Our books tend to be
hopelessly out of date. Magazines are a better bet for
current information.'

'I know there's at least one magazine devoted to it.
Do you have it?'

'Yes, and no. I've got it, but if you're in a
hurry—Gunnar Gustafsen took out the last two years'
issues last week.'

She had to wait until nine to call Gunnar. Damn.
The interview was tomorrow. She hadn't much time.

'Gunnar? I thought you had left town?'

'Hi, Kristy, love. No, I don't actually leave until
next week, but there was no way I could do that night
school thing. By the way, I am sorry about that. How
are you making out with Blake?'

'Blake?'

'Harding. He's in that class, isn't he? We're buddies.
I had him in a class last year—I was running to keep
ahead of him, I can tell you.'

'I'm running, all right,' she muttered. 'But I didn't
call you about the class, Gunnar. I'm trying to get
myself up to date on the latest networking systems—in
the next twenty-four hours—and it seems you've got
all the magazines out of our library.'

'I'll have them back on Monday. I'm researching it
myself—have to. The Montreal office is networked up
to its ears. Look, you could save yourself some reading
by calling Harding. He's set up that whole Canning
operation—had to do an extensive feasibility study
first. He's probably still got it all at his fingertips.'

'No, I——Could I borrow the articles, Gunnar? I've
got an interview tomorrow afternoon—I'm going for
Jack's job—and it seems one member of the selection
board is hung up on modernising our networking
system.'

'I'm sorry, Kristy, but I can't spare them today.

How about meeting for breakfast tomorrow? At my place. My wife can keep us supplied with coffee and I can give you a quick and dirty course on UNIX. Seven o'clock tomorrow?'

'Thanks, Gunnar. You're a doll. Whoops! Got to run. I've got a programming class starting in about ten seconds!'

Teaching new programmers was hard work at first, leading them through the early stages of confusion and bewilderment to this threshold. Then came the pay-off, the day when she suddenly found she was standing, watching the computer lab, and no one had called for help in at least five minutes.

They'd forgotten her, forgotten the world itself. It wouldn't last. In a few minutes one of the computers would reject something with the infuriating message 'Syntax error' and she'd be appealed to for advice.

But the nature of her role had changed for them. She had been the leader, guiding them into a strange world. Now it was their world, too. They were comfortable with the computers, working with them, and Kristy had dropped into the background.

The buzz of the telephone went unnoticed in the flurry of computer programming and debugging.

'Computer lab,' Kristy announced quietly.

'Good morning, Kristy.'

His voice was low and intimate. Last night his eyes had gone cold with fire. This morning he reached for her through the telephone. Much more of this and she'd have a complex about telephones.

'Are you all right, Kristy?'

'Yes, of course I am. Why?'

'You didn't answer your phone last night.'

'I didn't want to.' She was amazed to hear him laugh. 'I still don't want to.'

'I drove by this morning. I didn't see your car.'

'Because it wasn't there.' In a minute someone

would look up, needing her help at a computer. In a
minute——

'Were you with him?'

She stared over the computers at a girl outside,
walking hand in hand with her man. The girl was one
of her students. She didn't recognise the man.

'Kristy, were you?'

'No.'

She thought she heard him let out a long breath.

'Are you in love with him, Kristy?'

'That's none of your business.'

'No, of course you aren't,' he realised, his voice
growing in confidence. 'If you were, you'd have gone
to him last night. I was afraid you had—that you
loved him——'

'It's a good thing I don't. If I did, what you did
last night could have blown my life apart.'

'Kristy, I want to see you. Tonight.'

'No, not tonight. And not tomorrow.' She hung up.
Again. Was she going to spend her life hanging up on
Blake?

He would call back. Thirty seconds for him to redial
and get back through the switchboard. She started for
the door.

'Jenny, would you look after the phone. Take a
message if anyone wants me.'

'Sure thing!'

It started ringing again as Kristy walked through
the door. She kept walking.

She found Corrine on the switchboard, her freckled
face breaking in a smile as she saw Kristy.

'I just put a call through to you. Hold on, I'll get
him back here.'

'No!'

Corrine glanced up again, her hand frozen over the
keyboard.

'Are you sure? It was the same man that just called

a few minutes ago—sexy voice, sounded like a real hunk?'

'That's the one,' Kristy agreed wryly. 'I take it you'd recognise his voice if he called again?'

'That's for sure! Some of them just growl at me. He was very pleasant. There! The light's gone out. He's just hung up.'

'He'll call again,' predicted Kristy. 'When he does, would you put him through to 311?'

'You mean 371? The computer lab?'

'No, I mean 311. Any time he calls—today, tomorrow, next week—transfer him to 311.'

Corrine giggled. 'You're not serious? Extension 311 doesn't go anywhere.'

'I know that. That's just where I want him—nowhere.'

Corrine shook her head sadly. 'This guy sounds like every girl's dream. I——'

'Will you do it?'

'Oh, I'll do it, but I think you're crazy. David Roswell could never sound half so sexy as this one.'

A comment like that didn't even deserve an answer.

Back in the computer lab, Jenny gave her a message to call a Mr Harding.

She crammed the paper with Blake's number into the pocket of her skirt. Later, she dropped it into the wastepaper basket in her office.

She went back to her class, spent the afternoon deeply involved in her work. She didn't go to lunch, didn't see David except briefly in the hallway. Corrine slipped into her office during lunch.

'He keeps calling. Are you sure, Kristy?'

'311. Just keep sending him to 311.'

If she could only switch her thoughts off as easily as Corrine could switch Blake's voice.

But the next personal phone call she received wasn't from Blake. It was her father.

'I'm at the airport,' he announced, not bothering to identify himself.

'Will you be here long?' She fully expected he wouldn't. He sometimes paid flying visits to Vancouver without even calling her.

'Just overnight. How about dinner tonight? At the Georgia? Seven o'clock?'

'I'd love to. I'll meet you there.'

It would take her mind off the interview. If her father left her early, she might stay downtown and take in a movie before she went home.

She was working on a new course outline in her spare block when David knocked on her door.

'Come in.'

He stood by her desk, staring down at the papers she'd been working on.

'Is that the new night course?'

'Hmm.' She wasn't very happy with the last paragraph. She frowned at it, wishing he'd waited another five minutes before interrupting her. 'Are you going to sit down?'

'I guess so.' He didn't; didn't meet her eyes either. 'I was thinking you might call me.'

'Oh?'

He picked up the top page and started reading it. She resisted the urge to grab it back from him.

'That's not finished, David. I'll let you have a look at it when I've revised it, if you like.' He dropped the paper.

'Do you want to tell me about him?' he asked abruptly.

'Not particularly.'

'If you and he had something going—as long as it's over—I can accept that.'

'That's big of you. We have nothing going. Never did and never will.'

'All right.' David moved her briefcase out of the

way and sat in the chair she had offered him. 'Shall we have dinner at my place tonight? I thought we could take in a movie later, then——'

'My father's in town. He just called and we're meeting for dinner.'

'All right.' He was on his feet again. 'Next Wednesday?'

'Maybe we should leave it for a while, David. After the other night, I've gone off men for a bit. I think I'll concentrate on my job.'

'Look, Kristy, I might have given you the wrong impression last night. I guess I might have seemed to be pretty heavy-handed—'

'No, David.' She smothered a laugh. David, heavy-handed? 'I suspect you're almost too understanding. It makes me wonder what could have gone wrong with your marriage.'

He shrugged uncomfortably. 'She was—she's nothing like you, Kristy. She cared almost too much. It stifles a man, being clung to as if he were a life-raft instead of a person.'

Did it? Was that how Blake had felt the night she turned sixteen?

'I guess I should leave you to your work. I've got to get back to my communications class—I left them working on their public speaking assignments.'

'Thanks for stopping in, David.'

'We are still friends, aren't we? I value your friendship, Kristy.'

'Of course we're still friends.' But not lovers, she added silently. He may not realise it yet, but there would be no more Wednesday nights for her and David. 'By the way, I've applied for Jack's job.'

'I—oh. Well, good luck on it.'

She got in another ten minutes' work before the telephone interrupted her with the double ring that signalled an outside call.

'Kristy Murdock,' she announced, pencilling in a correction to the last sentence.

'What the devil did you tell that idiot of a switchboard girl to do with my calls?'

'How did you get past her?'

'I had my secretary place the call. After a whole day of calling, listening to the phone ring and ring——It's hard to believe there can be a telephone in a college that won't get answered eventually. Your switchboard operator is really a friendly girl. She never lost patience, but didn't seem to have any idea where you could be if you weren't answering your phone. Don't you have regular classes in that place? One call, I let it ring for half an hour. Where was I switched to? The furnace room?'

'I don't know.'

'You can do better than that, Kristy. Now tell me.'

She laughed. 'It's true. I don't know where it was ringing. I told Corrine to put you through to extension 311.'

'And what is extension 311?'

'Who knows? When they put in this telephone system—it's one of those new computer controlled set-ups—they allocated extension 311 to the storeroom where we keep our old textbooks. We use that room for an extra office sometimes when things get hectic here. The trouble was, when you dial 311, it doesn't go to that room. Nobody knows where it does ring —somewhere in the midst of the computer's brain, I guess. It's never been answered yet.'

'It was you I was calling. Not the telephone company's computer.'

'I didn't want to talk to you.'

He was laughing, too. 'I did realise that. You're one heck of a woman, Kristy. Unforgettable.'

'You managed to forget me easily enough—twelve years ago.'

'Not for more than a week or two at a time. You've been haunting me for years.'

'I don't believe that. You couldn't get away from me fast enough.'

'Surely you——No, this is not the time for this conversation. If I say the wrong thing, you'll hang up on me, you witch! Have dinner with me tonight?'

'I'm busy.'

'David Roswell?'

'It's none of your business who I'm seeing.'

'Everything about you is my business.'

'It's nothing to do with you. And Wednesday night —you had no right to come bursting in like that, pretending——'

'I know. I know I hadn't the right. But I will have the right, Kristy.'

'Retroactively?' she snapped.

'Yes,' he agreed. 'Retroactive to the day I met you again.'

'You're impossible! Do you have any idea how you're messing up my life?'

'I'm going to be your life,' he told her softly.

'No! I don't want——'

'Don't you? That's not the message I got when I kissed you last weekend. You remember? On the grass, not far from where we started to make love the night——'

'Stop it, Blake! Can't you just leave me alone? I don't want this. I don't want an affair. I don't want a marriage!'

'You will.'

'You've got the wrong woman. Marriage, children; Blake, I don't know anything about being a wife, or a mother. I'd make a mess of it all. I'm a career girl. It's all I know.'

'I have no intention of leaving you alone, Kristy. I made that mistake twelve years ago when you wouldn't see me the morning you left Saltspring Island.'

The door opened. Wilma came in, looking apologetic as if she knew this was a private conversation.

'What would change your mind?' she asked him. Wilma sat down and started sorting through her briefcase.

'Have dinner with me tonight. Stop running. Face what's between us honestly.'

'And then you'll go away?'

'I'll think about it.' That wasn't exactly a promise. 'I might take a lot of convincing.'

'Remember that cliff you took me up? When we were kids?'

'I remember it.'

'I should have pushed you off.'

He only laughed. 'How would you have got down without me? Now, about tonight——'

'Not tonight. My father's in town. I'm meeting him for dinner.'

'I'll join you. Where——?'

'No!' She quelled an irrational panic at the thought of the two of them seated across from her. Alone against the only two men who'd ever had power to hurt her. If they united together against her—'Not tonight.'

'Will you be home afterwards? I'll phone you.'

'I don't know.'

'Kristy?'

Wilma had stopped pretending not to listen. Kristy met her eyes across the small office.

'What?' she asked Blake.

'When you get home, plug your phone back in.'

She drew a doodle on the corner of the new course proposal.

'All right.'

CHAPTER SIX

BLAKE couldn't remember Verne Murdock clearly enough to recognise him, but he remembered what kind of man he was—immaculate, well-groomed, a social climber conscious of his image.

There were a lot of places a visiting executive might choose to take his daughter to dinner, but this executive would want to be seen by the right people. That narrowed the choice.

A businessman's visit to the coast. Afternoon meetings, followed by drinks at a quiet bar to put a seal of alcohol on whatever had transpired earlier at the office. Blake doubted if Murdock would be free for a social dinner before seven in the evening. When he was free, he was likely to choose a restaurant close to his hotel.

Before he left the office, Blake had Sonia phone the downtown hotels until she found which one Verne Murdock had registered in. Then, at seven-thirty, he started his search. As usual, he left his car behind to avoid getting tied up in Friday night's West End traffic jam.

He approached this search with the deliberate determination he gave to his work. He didn't expect to find Kristy right away; he wasn't surprised when the first two restaurants he tried produced nothing. Once he was hailed by a business associate, invited to join what looked like a lively party. He smiled and shook his head.

He passed Brenda Guest and her father as he was leaving the second restaurant.

'Evening, Winston . . . Brenda.'

'Join us, Blake?' Winston asked. Brenda looked away after meeting Blake's eyes for a reproachful instant.

'Not tonight.'

'Brenda phoned me today,' his mother had announced in a surprise visit to his office that afternoon. 'She was crying. She said you'd told her you were marrying another woman.'

'Oh?' The night before, Brenda had greeted his announcement with silence.

Blake had shifted uncomfortably under his mother's scrutiny. 'There didn't seem any point in letting Brenda think——She might have had reason to believe I was thinking of marriage—with her. I'm not. Not any more.'

His mother had stared at him silently, waiting for more.

'And?' she had asked finally. 'Are you planning to invite me to this wedding of yours?'

He had grinned then, his unaccustomed diffidence replaced by a mask of confidence.

'First, Kristy has to agree to it. Right now, she's doing a good job of resisting.' He had started prowling his office, frustrated by the memory of his recent conversations with Kristy.

'You've seen Kristy? How is she? I talked to her on the phone the other day. She sounded exhausted.'

'Did she? She seemed fighting fit to me. She's determined that she's a liberated lady, and I'm the male chauvinist——'

'Pig?' his mother had finished. 'Surely she didn't go so far as to call you a pig?' His mother had choked on what might have been a laugh, then sobered suddenly. 'Blake, do go carefully with that girl. This idea of yours—well, it seems like such a sudden thing. Surely you can't blame her for being wary. I can't

imagine she has a very positive attitude to marriage—her parents certainly haven't given her a shining
example of the joys of married life.'

'I know that, but—damn it! She's driving me crazy!
When she was younger, I was too damned young—or
stupid—to keep in touch when she left. Then, when I
realised how much I missed her . . . '

'You've been in love with Kristy all these years?
Why did you never go looking for her?'

'I thought of it sometimes, but I was sure that I'd
find her with someone else—married.'

'And now?'

'She wants me to leave her alone. But if I do
that——I made that mistake twelve years ago. I'm
not doing it again. Somehow, I've got to——Mother,
she's got a wall around her a foot thick! Somehow, I
have to get through it! If I let her walk out of my life
again, I'll be . . . ' Alone for ever, he had finished in
his mind, but he had said, ' . . . I'll miss her.'

'When are you seeing her?'

'She's having dinner with her father tonight.'

'Verne,' his mother had said, frowning.

Blake remembered, high on a cliffside, a younger
Kristy's confidences.

She had worshipped her father, had hung much of
her hopes for the future on the firm belief that living
with her father would give her a home, surround her
with love.

'I want a home like you have, Blake,' she had told
him, making him wish he could somehow protect this
child from disillusionment. 'You don't need two
parents for a home, do you? Maybe just one is better
sometimes. My Mom and Dad—they're so busy hating
each other, it doesn't leave them time to love me.
When Daddy moves east, I'm going with him. It'll be
better then.'

Remembering his brief meetings with her parents,

Blake wondered why they had allowed her to choose where she would live. For Kristy's sake? Or because neither of them really wanted her?

He wasn't sure just why he had decided to gatecrash Kristy's dinner with her father. To take advantage of any chance to see her, or to protect her? He was sure he hadn't imagined the tension in her voice when she mentioned her father.

He recognised Kristy's fabulous crown of red curls in the third restaurant he tried.

What a contrast they made—Kristy with her mobile, passionate face and her fountain of curls flowing freely down her back; her father with his sleek greying hair and cold blue eyes.

When Blake touched the back of her chair, Kristy looked up quickly, an inexplicable alarm growing in her eyes.

'Take it easy,' he urged her quietly, responding to her panic instinctively without knowing its cause.

'I don't know if you remember me from Saltspring Island,' he introduced himself to her father with swift confidence.

The older man made a swift professional connection. 'Harding? With Harding and McKay?'

'That's right.'

'You did that proposal for the Canning property development, didn't you? Are you alone tonight? Why don't you join us for dinner?'

'There's nothing I'd like better,' Blake agreed, returning Kristy's angry glare with a smile, slipping into the empty chair across from her.

How like him, she thought bitterly; joining her father, the two of them side by side, together. She watched him giving a drink order to the waiter, wryly watched her father deciding this was a contact he wanted to pursue.

Of course he didn't remember meeting Blake all

those years ago. Kristy remembered. It had been at her birthday party, one of her father's few appearances. Kristy had towed Blake over to her parents' side, hoping to impress her father with Blake. It hadn't worked. Her father hadn't seen Blake with her rose-coloured glasses.

Things had changed. They operated in the same world now. Blake's contact with the millionaire, Canning, made him irresistible to her father.

'We're making a bid on that project,' her father was confiding to Blake. 'In fact, that's the reason I'm in Vancouver. I was to meet Canning's VP over dinner tonight. I just got into town when the meeting was cancelled.'

She should have known. He hadn't called because he wanted to see her; she was a last-minute substitute for a more important business engagement.

'That was your good luck, wasn't it?' suggested Blake. 'I'm sure you'll enjoy dinner with Kristy far more than a business meeting.'

'I'm concerned about putting this thing back together again. I had hoped to fly home on the midnight flight tonight.'

Kristy received the menu from the waiter thankfully, staring blindly at a selection of foods described in various languages.

He hadn't written, hadn't called to say he was coming to the west coast. If his business dinner hadn't been cancelled, she would never have known he was here.

Heaven knew, she'd had enough opportunity in the past to learn that her father's affection for her was a leftover, if and when he had time for her. She came last, after all the other obligations.

It didn't really matter, hadn't mattered in years. Even now, he was more interested in pursuing business contacts with Blake than saying hello to his daughter.

She let their voices wash over her, ignoring the words. The words weren't important. The men weren't important. Let them pursue their priorities. After a while they would smile kindly at her and talk the kind of nonsense they thought she wanted to hear.

Kristy knew her place in her father's world. On the fringes.

'Do you get out here often?' Blake was asking. Why? Were they planning to do business together?

'A few times a year. My firm keeps me pretty busy in the Metro Toronto area. Most of their interests are there, although lately we've been expanding west.'

It sounded as if the nature of her father's job had changed over the years. It was the first indication Kristy had had from him. Not surprising. She hadn't seen him for almost a year.

'Give me a ring next time you're in town, Verne. I'm sure my mother would like to have you and Kristy to dinner. You'll come, won't you, Kristy?'

'I'd like to see your mother,' she evaded.

'I'd welcome the opportunity to meet some of your colleagues,' hinted her father, exchanging business cards with Blake.

'Oh, I think just family would be nicer. I try not to bring work home if I can help it. If you do want to discuss business, why not call my office and make an appointment to meet there?'

Kristy choked on her wine. Blake had delivered that so smoothly that her father hadn't even realised he'd been slapped down, ever so politely.

Kristy might not have realised either if she hadn't been watching Blake, seen the look in his eyes.

Her father was smoothly determined to talk about the Canning development; Blake effortlessly avoided making any statement the older man could take as inside information. Professional ethics, Kristy decided wryly. Blake was protecting his client's confidentiality.

They moved on to talk about the latest government budget speech and Kristy's silence ended. This was a subject she was vitally interested in.

'That's a typical easterner's viewpoint,' she accused her father at one point. 'You're ignoring everything west of the lakehead. The industrial east takes resources from the west—you've got to put something back.'

She was getting into this argument, shaking her hair back, getting ready for a serious dispute.

The motion caught her father's attention.

'Girl, when are you going to get that mop cut? You look like a refugee from the sixties—the hippie generation. It's a mess, never tidy.'

She couldn't stop her hands making a futile attempt to smooth the unruly waves.

'I'm not a tidy person.'

'I think Kristy's hair is the most beautiful thing I've ever seen,' said Blake quietly, forcing her to meet his eyes.

'Isn't that Canning at the entrance?' her father asked suddenly. 'I believe he's coming this way.'

Earl Canning moved in an aura of wealth and power. The man with him was obviously a business associate, but a junior one. Canning moved away from his companion when he saw Blake.

'Blake, so this is your mysterious dinner date.'

She lifted her after-dinner drink slowly to her lips. In a minute this man would join them, and the whole thing would turn into a business conference. She smiled tightly as Blake introduced Canning.

'Won't you join us?' her father offered with suppressed eagerness. 'I'm with Henslaw—Geoffrey Henslaw Corporation,' he explained as Canning didn't respond. 'I had an appointment with your vice-president this afternoon. Unfortunately it was cancelled.'

'Oh, yes? Which vice-president?'

'Denver. William Denver.'

The millionaire grinned with unexpected humour. 'If I sit down, we'll talk business. Now, every time I try to talk business to Blake over a dinner table, he tells me to call his office for an appointment.'

'I'm sure we can make an exception tonight.' Kristy's father wasn't about to pass up a meeting like this.

'Well, Blake?' Canning raised his brows in an amused query. 'My vice-president walked out on me this afternoon—his wife's just having their first child, so he stood up Murdock here. I hope he apologised, Verne. Mind if we join you, Blake?'

'Feel free.' Blake offered Canning a chair. 'Kristy and I will leave you to it—you don't mind if I steal Kristy away, Verne? There's a movie we wanted to take in across the street.'

'Of course,' her father agreed.

When she looked back, her father was already deep in conversation. He hadn't even said goodbye.

Tomorrow she would write him a note, thanking him for dinner. She doubted if he would answer.

Blake's hand was on her arm, urging her forward as the light changed.

'My car's back here,' she resisted.

'But the cinema is over here.'

'Thank you for helping me get out of there, but I——'

'Don't let him hurt you, Kristy.' She was across the street now. She would have to cross back to get to her car.

'He didn't hurt me. I just——'

'Don't pretend with me, Kristy. I could see how it was, watching you with him tonight. You keep expecting he'll behave like a real father, and he keeps proving how selfish he is. Don't hurt yourself expecting warmth from a shallow man.'

'You're talking about my father! He——'

Blake stopped walking, earning himself an angry

reprimand from a windswept man who had to dodge around them.

'Pretend to anyone else you like, Kristy, but not to me. Neither one of your parents has ever taken the time to make a home for you. Don't expect me to admire them.'

She looked away from the understanding in those black eyes, found herself looking into the openly curious gaze of an elderly woman waiting for a bus. Damn Blake. He had always seen more than he should.

'Why did you let my father con you into introducing Canning?' He could easily have avoided that. She looked back up at Blake. All evening, she had been trying not to see him. Unwillingly, she found herself enjoying the dark handsomeness of his face, the masculine breadth of his shoulders. He hadn't been this broad when she was sixteen. For the first time, it occurred to her how young Blake had been the night of her sixteenth birthday. To her, he had been a man, strong and mature.

'Because he's your father.' His full lower lip tightened wryly. 'I'm not in love with the guy, but if he's going to be my father-in-law——'

'Blake, you've got to stop this marriage business! It's ridiculous! Marriage is the last thing on my mind.'

'Let's argue later. We don't want to miss the movie.'

'Don't we? Do you always change the subject when you don't like the way the argument's going? You——Blake, you're impossible! I shouldn't be laughing at you, I should be——Oh, let's go to the damned movie. To tell the truth, I was planning on a movie anyway.'

A gust of wind curled around them and Blake used his free hand to brush her hair gently away from her eyes. His voice turned husky. 'You're one hell of a beautiful woman—my woman.'

She pulled away from him, only to find her hand promptly caught again as he walked on towards the cinema.

'I'm not your anything! I'm not anyone's possession and I have no intention of going anywhere with you. Not if you're starting that again.'

'What are you going to do? There's a police car, right over there. Why don't you call him, tell him your problem? Yes, officer. This man is harassing me. He insists he wants to marry me.'

'Oh, sure——' She shook her head, then couldn't help an unwilling laugh. 'I can just see it. There you are, looking as respectable as anything in your suit and tie, the image of——And here I am with my hippie hairstyle.'

'That's nonsense! You have the most beautiful hair. So help me, if you do anything to tame it, I'll——'

'Blake, we're in two different worlds. Maybe the women in your world ask permission before cutting their hair. In my world, if I want to cut my hair, I'll cut it.'

'Cut it if you want. I remember it short when you were young. It certainly wasn't tame. I suspect that your hair is only a reflection of your true personality, wild and passionate.'

She cursed her fair skin for the blush that rose at his words. 'The wildness is anger. You make me furious. Every time I see you, I—I'm not normally like this. Most of the time I'm a calm, rational person who——'

'How dull. What about your David? Doesn't he bring out the wildness in you? Surely your lover——'

'That's none of your business. My private life is none of your business. As a matter of fact, my life isn't your business at all. I wish——'

'Hush, let's not argue in the cinema.'

'There you go again! Trying to get out of it by

changing the subject. It had better be a good movie.'

She let him fill her arms with a massive container of popcorn. He took her arm and led her down the aisle, and ushered her into a seat.

'Enjoying yourself?' his voice asked teasingly. She was shocked to realise that she was smiling.

'I'm plotting your downfall,' she snapped back.

How long had it been since she had felt so alive, so——

This was insanity. Letting herself get caught up in a senseless battle with Blake, having fun as if it were a game.

It was a good movie. Not earth shattering, or socially significant, but a silly, funny love story that had her laughing one minute and almost crying the next.

When the hero of the story took the heroine in his arms, she embraced him passionately, melting her lovely body against his. The camera faded to the next scene, leaving the audience in no doubt as to the outcome of the lovers' embrace.

'I've dreamed of doing that to you,' whispered a low voice in her ear.

'No,' she protested weakly. 'Please don't,' she whispered against his lips as they found hers in the darkness of the cinema.

His hand found the side of her face, brushing the tangle of hair gently away as he drew his fingertips along her cheekbone, holding her face gently as his lips brushed against hers.

His tongue slipped through the lips that moved so softly against hers. She felt her lips tingling, opening to him. Her tongue moved to touch his. Her head fell back weakly against the back of the seat as he deepened the kiss, taking her mouth possessively with his, moving his hand down to caress the soft skin of her neck.

She found her heart thundering in her ears, her eyes closing to shut out everything but Blake's lips on hers, his hand on her throat. His lips dragged away from hers and she heard his breathing, ragged, close to her ear.

'Kristy . . . '

'No.' It was only a whisper of protest. She could feel the heat of his hand on her neck. His fingers traced along the V of her neckline. Her breath went short, knowing that in a moment——

'Someone will see,' she whispered against his lips.

'There's no one close enough to see. I picked this spot very carefully.'

'You deliberately——'

'Well, I knew it was a love story.' His tongue invaded her mouth again and she found herself kissing him back, hard and deep, her arms around his neck, holding his head down to her, wanting more and more, closer and closer until the ultimate intimacy.

When his hand left her neck, she shuddered, feeling his touch before it reached the roundness that was her breast. His hand cupped the fullness and she felt, rather than heard, his groan as he encountered the stiffness of her brassière. 'I need to feel you,' he whispered as his lips found the softness of her neck. 'You have such beautiful, soft skin.'

His hand dropped to her waist, slipping under her sweater to trace heated fingers against the soft skin of her midriff. Then up, cupping her breast as it swelled against him. His fingers slipped under the fabric, stroking the heated flesh, finding the hardness that revealed her own arousal.

When his fingers found the front fastening, her swollen breasts sprang free for his hands to cover and possess.

His mouth found hers again as his fingers took possession of the hardness that was her aroused nipples, covering her gasp with a deep kiss.

'I want to kiss them,' he told her with a low passionate whisper close to her ear. 'I want to kiss your breasts. I want to see you. I've never really seen you, only in the dark.' And his mouth descended on hers in a deep, shuddering kiss that left her burning for him, needing his touch as she had never needed anything in her life before.

'Blake, please——' His hands enfolded her breasts again, squeezing the nipples with a gentle rolling motion that made her forget everything.

'You want it, too, don't you?' She felt, rather than heard, his question.

'Yes,' she confessed, seeking out his lips with her own.

'More than you want David when he touches you?' His low voice cut through the haze of passion in her mind, bringing her back with a jolt.

On the screen, the scene changed from night to day, throwing light across the darkened cinema.

Her eyes were open now; she could see the silhouettes of other watchers. Shuddering, she pushed at Blake's hands.

'Stop it. This is a cinema, not——'

'A bedroom?' he suggested huskily, pretending to work at pulling her clothes back into shape.

'Take your hands off me!' she hissed. 'You're not helping. Let me out!'

'I'll come, too. We'll go somewhere else.'

'You promised me a movie; I want to see it. Just give me a minute in the ladies' room to tidy up. Please, Blake.'

She was shaking when she pushed through the swinging doors into the foyer. She ignored the knowing look from the girl serving popcorn. In the privacy of the Ladies she pulled her small brush through her hair, smoothing the wild disarray his hands had caused.

Her lips were bare of lipstick, kissed to a flushed fullness. She couldn't seem to get her mouth straight, couldn't get rid of the look of love-kissed vulnerability.

She remembered Blake's hands on her breasts, felt the muscles in her neck slacking with desire. She had wanted to let her head drop back, roll her head back and forth against the seat as his touch invaded the very core of her being.

She was almost thirty, yet she'd just been behaving like a teenager. Being seduced in the dark corners of a cinema.

No, she denied silently. As a teenager, she had never come so close to losing control. When her dates had kissed her in the dark, she had known exactly what she was doing. She had known exactly when to tell them to stop.

Except once. With Blake.

Blake. If she let him, he would force himself to the centre of her life, then leave her alone and cold in the darkness.

He was there in the foyer. He had followed her, was waiting for her to come out. He was talking to the girl behind the kiosk, probably learning that Kristy had indeed gone into the ladies' room.

Neither Blake nor the girl saw her slip through the unmarked doorway at the end of a short hallway.

She found herself in a corridor of offices. She started towards the red exit sign at the far end.

'Looking for someone?'

He looked as if he might be the owner, or some kind of manager—perhaps the accountant.

'The exit—I'm just looking for the exit.'

'Back the way you came! That way,' he repeated as she edged further along the hallway. 'This isn't a public area.'

'The usher said I could go out this way,' she lied,

moving quickly, conscious of his suspicious eyes on her all the way to the exit. She pushed open the door and escaped into the darkness outside.

Necking in darkened cinemas; sneaking through forbidden corridors to hide from a tall, dark man. Her life was turning into a twisted soap opera.

'Tune in tomorrow for the next episode in the life of Kristy Murdock,' she muttered, finally finding a street sign, then locating the tall black mass of Eatons' tower in front of her.

She drove home with her brain on automatic pilot, somehow escaping disaster in the Friday night traffic. She felt better inside, with her doors locked around her.

She plugged the phone back in, then got herself a cup of coffee and sat in the living-room, waiting for the telephone to ring. He would call, and it would be better, easier to talk to him on the telephone.

She picked it up on the first ring.

'One of these days,' he told her softly, 'you're going to realise that living life is easier than running away from it.'

'One of these days, you're going to realise that wanting something doesn't give you ownership.'

'I'm not the only one who wants. You couldn't hide that from me tonight, Kristy. In that cinema——'

'That was only sex. You're an attractive man and——'

'I'm glad you think so. Have lunch with me tomorrow. I'll be at the college. We can——'

'Shut up! You've got an ego the size of this city! I don't want a relationship, Blake. I admit that I'm attracted to you—I can hardly deny it after tonight—but I don't want to get involved with you.'

'Why not?' His voice dropped lower. 'Why did you run away, Kristy?'

'I——Because things were getting out of control.'

'Things?'

'Stop laughing at me!'

'Come on, Kristy! You're supposed to be an emancipated, modern girl. What a euphemism!—*things* were getting out of control!'

'You know what I meant!'

'I can hear you laughing, love. It's in your voice. Yes, I know what you meant. But do you, Kristy?'

'What do you mean?'

'What is it you're afraid of, Kristy?'

She looked down at her free hand, lying clenched in her lap. Below it, she was still dressed in the skirt she had worn to dinner with her father. She'd dressed up for him, put on a mask.

'You. I'm afraid of you, Blake. This is not a game. Someone could get hurt.' She concentrated on making the hand relax. 'I could get hurt.'

He was silent a long moment before he answered, 'So could I, love. Is that why you've closed yourself into that sterile life of yours?'

'It's not sterile, Blake. It can be exciting. There's a lot of warmth, a lot of caring that goes on in teaching. And I love being in the middle of it, seeing the changes going on all around me. You must understand that. I've watched you at night school, seen you getting involved in conversations with the others. It catches you up, too. You love your work; allow me the same privilege.'

'Kristy, my work is not a shelter, a safe place where I hide from living. That's what yours is, isn't it? As long as you can give them what they want, your students won't turn on you, won't reject you.'

'As long as—that's a funny way to put it, Blake.'

'But it's true, isn't it?'

'Maybe. Partly.' She smoothed her hand over the skirt, closed her eyes. Her fingers were hurting where they had gripped the receiver. She shifted it to her other hand.

'What are you wearing, Kristy?'

'The same thing I was earlier.'

'The rust-coloured skirt and blouse?'

'Yes. And a gold chain——'

'With a gold seashell hanging from it? Why didn't you change into something more comfortable?'

'I thought you might come here after the cinema.'

'And you wanted to keep your armour on?'

She laughed. 'Yes, whatever good it does me. It wasn't much help in the cinema.' She tucked her feet up under her, feeling crazily at home talking to him like this on the telephone.

'You looked gorgeous tonight. Where did you get the chain, Kristy? And the shell? Did David give it to you?'

'You've got a bit of a complex about David, haven't you?'

'I've been wondering all evening, ever since I first saw that chain around your neck. It's the kind of thing a man would give a woman he——Would you wear another man's gift when you came to see me, Kristy?'

'I wasn't coming to see you; I was having dinner with my father. And you've no right to be jealous.'

'Rights have nothing to do with it, my dear. Are you still seeing him?'

'Still? Do you remember last night? You put a bit of a spanner into any relationship I might have had with David.'

'Might have had?'

'It was on the way out anyway, Blake. He and I, we were comfortable together, but there wasn't any more than that.' Her fingers were playing with the gold shell at her neck. 'I didn't want there to be any more than a romantic friendship. And he didn't give me the shell. I never let him give me anything—except dinner, and once an umbrella to replace one he'd borrowed and lost. I got the shell in Mexico last year.'

'I don't know that I care for the sound of that romantic friendship. Mexico, you said. When? Last summer?'

'Yes.'

'The west coast or the east coast?'

'The east coast.' She named the village where she had stayed.

'Did you go to the beach? Kristy, I was only miles away, at the next village. We could almost have passed each other on that beach. Did you see the young Mexican fellow with the horse?'

'Yes! He came to the beach every morning, early. He was training the horse. The two of them would run through the sand. It was beautiful, watching that magnificent stallion, and that brown boy—they worked together as if they were soulmates. Blake, did you go to the markets? Aren't they fabulous? All the people selling their wares; the noise and the colour!'

His laugh was deep over the phone. 'Fabulous, isn't it? I hardly spoke any Spanish, though, so I know I missed a lot of what was happening. I've been taking Spanish lessons, practising on my secretary—she speaks excellent Spanish. Let's go back, Kristy. You have holidays soon, don't you? I heard you telling Marion your holiday plans had fallen through.'

'In about two weeks. I was going to go to San Francisco, but—I might go out to mother's house, put it in shape for the sale.'

'Come with me instead. We'll go to San Francisco, then on to Mexico. We'll go back to the village where you stayed before, spend a couple of weeks just soaking up the sun and playing. Wouldn't you like that, Kristy?'

'Yes, but Blake—Mexico is——' It was a special

place to her. She'd gone alone, been entranced by the country. Sharing it with Blake seemed somehow dangerous, yet tremendously tempting.'

'I'll make the reservations, Kristy. Two weeks from Saturday. How's that?'

'No, I—I've got this job I'm doing for my mother.'

'What job?'

'Her office system. She asked me to do it.'

'Wouldn't you rather come to Mexico?' His voice was seducing her.

'Yes, but I'm terribly afraid I'd regret it.'

'You won't. I promise you.' He sounded so persuasive.

'Blake, if I go, it's not a commitment. We're talking about Mexico, not marriage.'

'We'll see.'

'Stop laughing at me! You've got to take this seriously. You're so used to having your own way, but you can't in this. I'm a career girl, Blake. My career means everything to me.'

'Everything, Kristy?'

'It's not just teaching. Teaching these last few years, I've got a lot of ideas about how the college could improve what it's doing. If I had the power to put them into effect, I think I could do something really worthwhile. I've applied for my boss's job, Director of Business Education. I'm being interviewed tomorrow. If I get it——'

'You? You can't apply for that job, Kristy!' She tensed at the sudden harshness of his voice.

'I already have. You can't stop me, Blake; the cave man bit went out years ago. There's really nothing you can do to stop me.'

'You're wrong, Kristy. I can stop you. Tomorrow afternoon I can stop you.'

'What do you mean?'

'If you're being interviewed tomorrow afternoon, I'll be there, too.'

'You can't just—Blake, don't tell me that you——' She began to put together details that had lain dormant in her mind every since Jack asked her to take on the night-school class Gunnar had deserted. 'You're on the advisory board, aren't you? You're the board member who's all hot to trot on getting Unix into the college? Gunnar told me you were up on Unix. And Jack told me there was a board member in that night-school class, but I didn't know the name.'

'Now you know.'

'You can't sit on that board, Blake. You're biased.'

'I'm biased, all right. But I'll be there. You're not getting that job, Kristy. You're going to marry me.'

She closed her eyes tightly, her heart pounding with panic. She whispered, 'You keep saying you want to marry me.'

'I'm going to marry you.'

She opened her eyes again, stared as if she could see him. Tonelessly, she said, 'What's in it for me?'

'What do you mean?' For once, he seemed startled, almost uncertain.

'What have you got to offer me?' she asked harshly, welcoming the growing anger. 'Marriage? That's nothing, just a piece of paper, a few words said in a church or a register office. Pain and trouble, that's all marriage is! Are you offering love? Friendship?'

'You know how I feel about you.'

'Yes, I guess I do! You want me; a possession, that's what you want. It's not love. What kind of love could that be? My dreams, my desires mean nothing to you. Marriage terrifies me, but that doesn't stop you pushing at me. I love my work, but you'll destroy it without a thought. You want children, so I'll have children whether I can handle it or not! You——'

'Kristy!'

'I wouldn't dare let myself love you! You'd take everything, leave me with nothing of my own!' She fell silent, exhausted by her own anger. For once, he was silent.

After a moment, she said, 'Goodnight, Blake.'

He said nothing.

CHAPTER SEVEN

CORRINE rang through to the classroom just before two.

'They're ready for you, Kristy, in the boardroom.'

'Thanks.'

'Good luck. My money's on you.' Corrine's voice dropped to a whisper. 'I was just in there and I overheard Mac saying that our Jonathan was a good man. Jack winced, and the dark fellow said, "If you want to turn the clock back fifty years, he's your man." I'll swear I've heard his voice before. Is he——?'

'Thanks, Corrine. I'd better get in there.'

She would have been scared in any case, but this was like going into the arena to fight the lions with her bare hands. There was no way she could win if Blake was determined to defeat her. But if he was going to vote against her, she was going to make it as hard as possible for him.

'Miss Murdock.' Dr McAllister nodded a courtly head towards the far side of the table.

It was a round table, the three of them lined up in an arc across from her. Blake watched her come into the room as if she were a stranger. She sat down, glad that her knees held up long enough to get her to the chair.

'You've met Mr Harding?'

'Yes. He's in my night-school class.' She couldn't help a slight smile as she said that. It was crazy, being interviewed by one of her students.

Blake said nothing.

Jack had a copy of her résumé in his hand. 'Kristy,

117

we'll start by going over some points in your background. You've been teaching at this community college for three years now. Before that, you were doing systems analysis in Toronto?'

'That's right.' She named the firm she had worked for, although he must have read it in her résumé.

'Tell us more about your duties in that job.'

Blake had heard some of this the night she introduced herself to the night-school class. Jack knew a lot of it as well, but he drew her out now, emphasising the supervisory nature of her duties, the administrative skills she had developed.

Whenever she looked at Blake, his eyes were elsewhere, yet she felt as if he were watching her intently.

McAllister leaned forward and interrupted Jack. 'I think we're clear on that area now, Jack. Miss Murdock . . . ' He hesitated, forming his words. 'You're a woman.'

She resisted a disastrous impulse to laugh. 'Yes, Dr McAllister.'

'Do you have any plans to marry?'

'No, I don't.'

His brows raised. 'Never, Miss Murdock?'

'I have no plans to marry, Dr McAllister. If I did decide to marry, I certainly wouldn't abandon my career. My work is very important to me, and I think I'm good at it. I think the community colleges have an important contribution to make to the people of this province and I'm not about to turn my back on Point Grey College for an underpaid position as a cook and nursery governess.'

Dr McAllister leaned back and stared at her. He looked astounded. Blake coughed in what she thought was an attempt to cover a bark of laughter until she heard his voice, deadly serious, asking, 'What do you see as the priorities for equipment in your department?'

'You mean future equipment? Capital expenditure?'

'That's right. Give it a five-year framework. What kind of equipment would you like to see?'

It didn't matter what she said. He was going to vote against her in any case.

'There's so much equipment we could use. Giving you a list of what I'd like wouldn't be very meaningful, unless we have the money to buy it. We have to be realistic. Money is very short. The Ministry has been cutting back severely on funds for capital expenditure. I think every dollar we get has to be used as effectively as possible.' She took a breath and plunged, describing the equipment she felt should be purchased over the next few years.

'What about networking?' he demanded. This would be how he looked in a business meeting, his face intent and stern.

'We're already networked. It's not the most up-to-date system, but I think it's good enough for some time to come.'

'Aren't you trying to train students for the real business world? Networking is what's happening out there.' Was he closing in for the kill now? His eyes had taken on a predatory gleam.

'Yes, but only part of what's happening. Our student load is increasing. With high unemployment, more people are enrolling, and we have an increasing number of employed people coming to upgrade their skills.' She went on to outline facts and statistics that were probably as familiar to him as they were to Jack and Dr McAllister. She was going to stay rational. He might disagree, but he'd know why she felt as she did. 'If we do what you're suggesting, it can only be after we've doubled the number of computer work stations.'

'You're operating on the assumption that the government is the only source of capital for your department. Aren't there a number of industries that have an interest in this aspect of education?'

'If we can solicit funds from industry, all the better, but we have to set up priorities. As Jack knows, I've already proposed modernising our network, but not as a top priority.'

When Blake had finished drawing her out on her ideas for expansion in the department, she felt as if she'd been through a wringer.

'You'll be notified,' Dr McAllister told her at the end. 'We have two other applicants to interview, and, as you no doubt realise, Mr Kinney has also applied.'

'When will the decision be made?' Some decision. The Principal didn't want a woman in the job because she might get married; Blake didn't want this woman in the job because he wanted to marry her, and she was opposed to his pet scheme. That left Jack—one out of three.

'Interviews will be complete on Monday. We'll make our decision after that. Thank you for your time, Miss Murdock.'

'How'd it go?' asked Wilma when Kristy reappeared in their office.

'Who knows. Mac would rather I had a beard. Thanks for looking after my class, Wilma.'

'They kept you long enough. You were in there over an hour. Jonathan only got thirty minutes.'

'That may not be a good sign. Anyway, all I can do now is wait and see.'

'There's a college social tonight—Board of Directors and other dignitaries meeting with the staff. You could go and try to curry favour.'

'No, I've had it. They either take me as I am, or forget it. I'm going for an exciting evening—grocery shopping, then home for a very instant supper.'

'No David?'

'No David. That's over—and don't speculate,

Wilma. I'm swearing off men. They're more trouble than they're worth.'

'Personally, mine's worth a lot of trouble, but I know I'm lucky. Before you start your exciting evening, Kristy, I'm afraid you'll have to spend some time in the lab. You know young Jenny? She put a disk in backwards or something. Anyway, it's jammed and the drive light won't go out. I turned the power off and put a sign on the computer to keep everyone away.'

After a half-hour of playing with the jammed disk, Kristy decided to go looking for a screwdriver and take the cover off the disk drive. It took another half-hour to find the right kind of screwdriver. She went down to audio-visual in the end and found a technician more than willing to have his screwdriver open her disk drive, so long as he was the man operating the screwdriver.

In the end, she gave him instructions and watched him spend thirty minutes doing a job she could have completed in ten.

She got out of the college at seven, drove to the nearest Safeway store and found it teeming with shopping trolleys and harrassed women. By the time she had wheeled her trolley into the car park, Kristy felt she had just completed an endurance run.

She dragged herself up the stairs to her apartment, shuffling two shopping bags around so that she could get her key into the lock. She had the key lined up, starting into the lock, when the door moved away from her and she almost fell into Blake's arms.

'What are you doing here? How did you get in?'

'I wanted to talk to you. Come on in. You're letting in the cold.'

He pushed the door shut behind her and took the bags away from her. She shoved her hands into her pockets and leaned back against the doorway, watching him walk towards her kitchen with the groceries.

'Take your coat off,' he invited.

'Whose apartment is this, anyway?' He ignored her tart question and she shrugged, too tired to pursue the matter. 'I've got more groceries in the car.'

'I'll get them.' He returned and started unbuttoning her coat. 'Give me your keys.'

'You're trying to manage me again,' she complained, but it hardly seemed to matter. She pulled the keys out of her pocket, then hesitated. 'How did you get in?'

He took the keys from her hand. 'I got in with a credit card. That's not much of a lock you have. You should have a locksmith in to install something more secure.'

'People don't usually try to break into my place; you're the first.'

'Get the locksmith anyway, just to humour me. Why don't you start unpacking those groceries while I bring the rest in. You could start us some supper. It's been one hell of a day. I could use a good home-cooked meal.'

'I'm not cooking dinner for you. If you want dinner served, go and pay for it, or go home and get your mother to cook it.'

'No, Kristy. I don't want to do either of those things. I want to spend some time with you.'

'You say that you've had a rough day, Blake? Well so have I. And you're part of the reason—most of it; you and Mac and an idiot down in audio-visual who's afraid he'll lose his masculinity if he lets a woman use his screwdriver. I'm tired. I've had it, and I'm not about to turn myself into a kitchen slave. If you want food here, cook it yourself. I'm going to have a hot bath.'

He'd probably be gone when she came out; he wasn't about to start cooking in her kitchen. Kristy grinned, thinking of that. She wouldn't be surprised to learn he'd never had his hands in dishwater in his life.

She locked the bathroom door and set the water pounding into the tub. It felt good when she got in, hot and soothing. She slipped down and leaned her head back against the bath pillow she'd picked up in a gift shop. She closed her eyes, told herself she was forgetting he was in her apartment.

Part of her kept listening for the sound of the door slamming, but of course he wasn't about to leave that easily. What she didn't expect was the smell of steak frying.

The smell was even stronger when she came out of her bedroom, scrubbed clean and thoroughly wrapped in her green caftan from neck to ankles.

'You should always wear green,' Blake told her when she came into the kitchen.

He was cutting tomatoes on the worktop, keeping an eye on two big steaks sizzling in her electric frying pan.

'I didn't know you could cook.'

'I can't. See this little plate on the handle of your frying pan? That's the temperature it says for steak, so that's where I set it.'

'You're not doing badly for someone who can't cook. What about the salad?'

'This is not salad. It's sliced tomatoes and cucumber. If I manage to get those steaks out of the pan before they turn to charcoal, do you think I can stay for dinner?'

She laughed. 'Don't be so meek, it doesn't suit you. I guess you've earned supper, but, Blake, I don't want to talk about getting married, or——'

'And I don't want to talk about that job you're trying for. Do you think we could find another topic of conversation?'

'With the universe to choose from——'

'We're sure to think of something,' he agreed. 'Would I be out of line if I asked you to set the table? I know that you're a liberated lady, and I'm an unrepentant chauvinist, but I've opened every door in this kitchen and I haven't found a plate yet.'

'In the sideboard, in the dining area. You concentrate on the cooking; I wouldn't want to do anything to contribute to the ruin of those steaks. I'm starving.'

She set out plates and glasses, even got out a bottle of wine that had been in her cupboard since Christmas. She hesitated over the candles. Candlelight might give Blake ideas, but it would be nice to turn the lights down. She wouldn't have to work to keep a mask on her face. She was far too tired to fight, or to pretend, tonight. She lit the candles and switched the overhead light off.

'Good thinking,' Blake approved. 'Here's the food. Let's hope it's edible.'

'It's lovely,' she decided after the first bite. 'With the proper training, you might become a competent cook.'

'I'll keep that in mind.'

'Don't you ever cook for yourself in your apartment, or don't you actually live there?'

'I usually stay in town during the week, then go home to New Westminster at weekends.'

'What do you eat?'

'I've got a few tins in the apartment for emergencies, but I confess that I usually eat in restaurants. What about you? Do you eat here in solitary splendour?'

'Usually. Saturdays I have a guest for breakfast——' she saw his sudden glare '—no, that's not what I mean, Blake! You're bristling like an angry dog! Calm the wild beast within yourself; my guest is four years old. Denny, from downstairs. He and I have a pancake breakfast together most Saturdays.'

'And David? Since you brought up the subject.'

'I didn't—not really. And if we don't change it, we'll start fighting again, won't we? I'm not willing to fight over David.'

'You said once that he asked you to marry him.'

'He didn't ask me to cook meals. Or quit my job. And he knew how to take no for an answer. Not like some people I know. I thought we weren't going to talk about——'

'All right. Eat up your steak and I'll take you out for dessert at the Dairy Queen. I'll buy you a butterscotch sundae—is that still your favourite?'

'I haven't had a sundae in years, and I don't think I've ever been to a Dairy Queen. Are you reliving your childhood?'

'Perhaps. And you're going through premature old age. It's time you had a little fun, did a few things for no better reason than that you feel like it.'

'First we'd have to do the dishes.'

'They'll keep.'

'No, they won't. You're hoping they'll keep until after you're gone? You're not getting away with that, Blake. Just for tonight, you'll have to pretend you're a modern man. You had the fun of making the mess, now you can help clean it up.'

'Were you a slavedriver in a previous life?'

'Probably. That's why I got into teaching. I like telling other people what to do. How did you get into accounting?'

He shrugged. 'I don't really know. I was always good at maths. Business seemed the logical thing to go into. Accounting may sound dry, but it's the opener for a lot of exciting things.'

'Like being the inspiration behind that new project of Victor Canning's? And the Towers expansion?'

'You've been listening to gossip.'

'But it's true, isn't it? And I'm not scoffing—I think

it's wonderful. It may be a moneymaking project for Canning, but there'll be jobs created, won't there?'

'Some people can't see that. Yes, you're right, a lot of jobs—not just construction work, either; some of them are long term. All right, stop shoving dishes at me. I'll help with the washing up.'

Later, when they went out to her car, he took the keys from her. 'After burning the steaks and breaking one of your best glasses, don't I get to play the man of the family and drive the car?'

'If it makes you feel good, all right.' She sat silently beside him as he drove to the Dairy Queen. When they were seated across from each other in the brightly lit ice-cream parlour with calorie-laden ice-cream sundaes in front of them, she finally asked, 'Where's the catch? You're being wonderfully agreeable, hardly a sign of male aggression,' and watched him break into a grin. 'Don't laugh! This is the first time since I met you again when you've—I guess I can't help wondering what's going on in that mind of yours.'

'In short, you think I've got ulterior motives?'

'Yes. What are you up to, Blake?'

He stirred his ice-cream absently, staring down at it. Finally he looked back up to meet her eyes, grinning.

'I must be tired,' he admitted, 'but I just wanted to spend an evening with you, enjoy being with you without any of the complications.'

'But there are complications. Today you interviewed me for a job that you've told me you're going to make sure I don't get. Would you really do that, Blake?'

He swallowed a mouthful of ice-cream slowly, letting it slide down his throat in a cooling reflex.

'It would be a hell of a demanding job. You can't devote your life to a career like that—it's not natural, not right for you. You're a warm, passionate woman. Leave the careers for women who are cold and barren, need something to devote their lives to. You——'

'Blake, you're trying to make my choices for me. You're trying to tell me how to live my life, what goals to have.'

'I want to marry you, Kristy. I lo——'

'That's what you want, but what about me? You know, I love your mother very much, but she's spoiled you rotten. She's given you everything you've ever asked for, before you even asked. And I'll bet that you've found other women to do the same since you've grown up. There've been women, of course there have.'

'Are you jealous of them?'

'That's not the point. You've got that kind of sexy confidence that shows you have an easy time with women. I don't think you've ever had to stop and consider a woman's point of view.'

'And you, Kristy? Is what you've got better? You were a passionate, alive girl. That girl's still there, underneath, but she's freezing over. The life you're forcing yourself to live, without love, is drying you up. You've changed, Kristy. You're afraid of living now, afraid of loving.'

She looked down. The sundae wasn't as good as she'd thought it would be. 'Maybe that's true, Blake. Maybe I'm getting hard, and cold. But it is my life.' She took a deep, ragged breath. 'I wish you'd let me alone to live it on my own terms. I want to go home.'

'Now?'

'Yes.'

It was a silent ride. She didn't even argue about who was driving, but held out her hands for the keys when they arrived back outside her house.

'I'll unlock your door.'

'You're not coming in, Blake! I've had enough. You've said I'm a cold, barren spinster. All right. Just let me go to my cold bed in peace, without all this——'

'Kristy.' He turned her round, holding her shoulders and looking down through the darkness at her. 'I'm sorry. I didn't mean to say anything to hurt you. And I don't——' He shrugged, then abruptly pulled her towards him, lowering his head until their lips met.

She had felt cold, empty, but his lips touched hers with a spark of warmth that had her suddenly yearning for his arms, his skin against hers, for just the closeness of his presence next to her. If only——

'Blake?'

'Yes, darling?'

'Are you really going to stop me from getting that job? You wouldn't really do that, would you?'

His arms tensed around her, then slipped away. 'I don't know, Kristy. I honestly don't know what I'm going to do.' They stood staring at each other as a fine rain began to fall. 'I guess I'd better go,' he said finally.

'Yes,' she agreed, turning away to let herself into her empty apartment. She knew that she should have begged him not to speak against her to McAllister and Jack, but she found that she couldn't.

Kristy woke up the next morning to a small hand shaking her shoulder. 'Hmm?' She opened her eyes enough to see Denny's frowning face. 'What time is it?'

'Nine o'clock. You're still sleepin'.'

'Sorry, love. I'll get up in a minute.'

'There's a man here,' Denny announced matter-of-factly.

'A man? At the door?'

'In the kitchen. He says he can't cook pancakes, but he knows how to make coffee.'

Blake. How dared he!

'Don't you ever wait to be invited?' she demanded

as she stormed into the kitchen.

He grinned. 'Are you one of those women who snarls until she's had her first three cups of coffee? I was afraid of that. I've got the coffee on—coffee I can do. Actually, you may not believe it, but I usually make the first pot of coffee every day in my office.'

'Your secretary must figure you're something pretty special. She gets to do all your dirty work, and you make one pot of coffee.'

'You are bitchy, aren't you?'

'I am not! I—oh, Blake, what am I going to do with you? See what you've done? Here I am, shouting at you again, as if I were a fishwife. You're driving me to distraction!'

'Sounds promising.'

'I can assure you that it isn't. What are you doing here? Didn't we part last night on a——'

'Yes, we did.' He touched her hair, brushing it back from her face. His voice was oddly soft. 'You wouldn't like me to brush your hair, would you?'

'Is it a mess?' she asked, hypnotised by his eyes on her.

'I don't know. It's beautiful. Those curls—have you any idea how the light catches them? They look just like burnished gold.' His fingers were tangling in her hair, combing it back slowly so that the curls twisted around his hands.

'I'll cut it off and give it to you, then maybe you'll—why are you here, Blake? You know, most people come to the door and knock. Most people wait for an answer before they come in. Some people even phone to ask if it's convenient for them to visit.'

'If I phoned, would you invite me over?'

'Not if I had any sense.'

He shrugged. 'See?'

'Oh, you—you're impossible!'

'You know, I think all those derogatory remarks

you make about me are a promising sign.'

She giggled. 'If you really want me to work at it——'

'Can I stay for breakfast? Pancakes, you said? I haven't had pancakes in years. And after breakfast, we could go out. I brought my car, just to show you that I do have one. I thought you and Denny might like to go to Stanley Park.'

Denny's face lit up as Kristy said doubtfully, 'I don't know, Blake.'

'Stanley Park?' said Denny eagerly. 'Can I see the big bird this time, Kristy? The one that makes the funny noise?'

Blake raised his eyebrows. 'Big Bird? I thought that was a television character.'

'The emu. It's a great, monstrous bird they've got at the zoo. No wings. It stands about as tall as you do. It's from Australia, I think, or maybe New Zealand. We can't go, Blake. We'll just fight.'

'We can avoid all these contentious issues.'

'We tried that last night. It didn't work.'

'We were just practising. We'll do better this time.'

'I'll bet! No heavy conversations? No advances? You promise?'

'Don't restrict me too much. How about letting me make advances that Denny here could witness? Like this?' He bent to brush his lips across hers. 'Now go and change out of that sexy nightdress into something like a sexy, tight pair of jeans.'

'You've got *sexy* on the brain!'

He helped with the cooking and the dishes again, which might have seemed like a concession, but she had put on the jeans he suggested, and she seemed to have agreed to spend the day with him. Had she agreed? She didn't remember agreeing. Would she end up in Mexico with him the same way?

Kristy was frowning as she walked out to Blake's

car, but she wasn't alert enough to stop Blake from
guiding her into the front seat, beside him.

'I was going to sit in the back with Denny.'

'I'd rather have you beside me, right here.'

'I don't like being managed,' she muttered as he
settled his long frame into the seat beside her.

'Then co-operate,' he suggested.

'What you want and what I want are incompatible.
Why should I co-operate against my own best interests?'

'What's your best interest, Kristy?' asked Denny,
eager to take part in this obscure adult conversation.
Blake started to answer,

'Kristy's best——'

'Don't!' warned Kristy. 'If we're to spend the day
together, you've got to stop this. At least save it for
when we're alone.'

'If you promise me there will be a time when we're
alone.'

'You don't miss a trick, do you?'

'That's better. I like watching you smile.'

'I have to be careful every minute with you. If I
don't——'

'You've got it wrong. It's me that has to watch for
every opportunity. If I don't, you'll get that door
slammed in my face.'

'What door? There's no door between us right now.'

'Only the one in your mind.'

Denny pushed his head through the space between
the bucket seats, staring at Kristy curiously. 'How can
you have a door in your mind, Kristy? What do you
use it for?'

'For self-defence. See that truck, Denny? That's a
horse trailer on the back of it. See the horse?'

'Wow! That's a real horse, a big one!'

She needed that door in her mind. Without it, she
would be in Blake's arms. There was a traitor inside

her mind, urging her to relax, give in, let his arms take her where they wanted, let him have his way with her life.

She glanced at him. Lying in his arms at night, waking to Blake's face at her side. If only——

'Are we going to see the monkeys?' asked Denny.

'Yes, monkeys, of course,' agreed Kristy.

'And the killer whales, the bears and the emu,' added Blake.

Tigers would be more like it. She had a tiger beside her, stalking his prey.

She shuddered, remembering Denny's cat playing with a mouse it had stalked and no longer had an appetite for.

All of Vancouver seemed to have come for Saturday morning at Stanley Park Zoo. Parents and children and lovers were herded together, enjoying the sun and the green park, the enchanting outdoor zoo filled with an exotic assortment of animals. Denny ran ahead of Blake and Kristy, arriving at the place where he could lean over a cement rail to look down at the polar bears lazing on the rocks below.

'Watch out!' Kristy warned him, nervously reaching a hand to grab hold before he could go tumbling down into the pit below.

One spectator at the bear pit was less good-natured than most. He turned to leave, ramming into Blake, then shouting angrily, 'Watch where the hell you're going!' as he reeled past.

Blake dropped an arm around Denny's shoulders to draw him out of the way.

'Wow! He was mad!' marvelled Denny. 'You should o' thumped him out, Blake!'

'I can't go around thumping everyone who's had a few drinks too many. It would be a waste of time. When he sobers up, he wouldn't remember. Let's have a look at those monkeys now.'

'Why did you hit Dave?' Kristy asked suddenly.

'What?'

'Remember the summer you taught me to dive? One day you and Dave Bentley were up on the hillside. The rest of us were coming up from swimming. None of us heard what he said to you, but we all saw you hit him. You were furious. I've never seen you like that. At least——'

'I bet he was a bad guy,' Denny decided. 'Was he a bad guy, Blake?'

'Not exactly.' Kristy was intrigued to see Blake's discomfort. 'Why don't you go and get some peanuts to feed the monkeys, Denny? Kristy and I'll rest our feet for a while. We'll be sitting on the grass over there.'

'Denny's too young to go on his own,' Kristy protested. 'He'll get lost.'

'I won't get lost! I can get the peanuts.' He took the money from Blake's hand and set off for the kiosk before Kristy could succeed in changing Blake's mind.

'He'll be OK. We'll keep him in sight. All he has to do is stand in the queue and ask for peanuts. Any time he looks this way he'll see us.'

'I suppose it's all right.' She sank down on the grass, kicking her shoes off and enjoying the coolness against her feet. 'I get a bit panicky sometimes when he's with me. He's so small. I get frightened that he'll get hurt, or lost, or——'

'He's a pretty self-sufficient kid. He'll be in our sight every minute. There's really no danger, but he'll feel grown up because he's doing something on his own. He reminds me a lot of Luke when he was a few years younger.'

'Luke?'

'My partner's son—my godson. He's eleven years old. We spend a lot of time together.'

'What do you do together? Where do you go?'

'Oh, wherever.' He shrugged. 'It depends. When he was younger, we did this sort of thing—trips to the park. We're more ambitious these days—hiking, fishing.'

'Have you been out to Lighthouse Park? I love that park. It always seems so far away from the city, almost like being out on Saltspring Island. It's a wonderful place to recharge my batteries without having to go too far.'

'Then come with us. We'll go there tomorrow.'

'No, I couldn't.'

'You'd enjoy it. You'd like Luke.'

'I—no, Blake. I've promised to do some work for my mother. I'll be at her office all day.'

'I heard about that. Delia told me. Every night last week, Kristy. You're working too hard, love. You've got to——'

'Blake, you promised! Well, you said we wouldn't get into this kind of thing.'

'I can see signs of exhaustion. Your eyes are a giveaway, you know.'

'I like my work. It's important to me.'

'You can't make it a substitute for living. Tell your mother to call up a consultant and pay for it like everybody else.'

'Shall I tell her to call you?'

'Tell her to call the devil if you like. I'm not soliciting business. I'm concerned about you.'

'I want to do this.' He didn't contradict her lie, but she knew he wasn't convinced. 'I don't see Denny!' she panicked suddenly. 'He was in the queue, but I can't see him now!'

'He's there. Behind the big fellow with the motor-cycle helmet.'

Yes, he was there. 'You should have your own children,' she said. 'You're good with them. Denny can be quite stand-offish, but——' She fell silent at the look in his eyes.

'I'm willing,' he told her softly, 'but it does take two. I know there are women who decide to be single mothers these days, but it's a little different for a man.'

'A child should have two parents.' Denny had two parents. He was secure and loved. Anyone could see that, just looking at him.

'I think so, too.' He ran a finger down her bare arm. She jerked away from his touch.

'I didn't mean you and me!'

'I did. You want children. I've been watching you with Denny. You're no more content with living alone than I am.'

'You don't live alone. Your mother——'

'I spend weekends at home; most nights I'm alone in my apartment. But a mother is hardly a substitute for a wife, for a lover.'

'I don't want——'

'You're lying,' he accused her, watching her eyes as his fingers traced fire back up her arm. 'You do want . . .'

'No! That's just sex.'

'Just?' he turned her softly. 'The other night in the cinema I don't think you'd have said that.'

'You don't play fair, do you?'

'All's fair in love and war.'

'And which is this? Denny! Bring the peanuts over here! There's a squirrel here. If we try, we might get him to come up to us for a peanut.'

CHAPTER EIGHT

DENNY was all in favour of Blake's plan to take them for a drive out towards Point Grey.

'Spanish Banks,' suggested Blake with a grin. 'We could go for a walk along the beach.'

'Are you crazy? We're not taking Denny along there! It's the height of summer. It'll be full of nude sunbathers.'

He laughed. 'Prudish, aren't you? And I thought I was supposed to be the conservative one.'

'What's consa—what's that, Kristy?' Denny had found he could push himself through the space between Blake's bucket seats.

She looked at Blake and laughed. 'I don't think I can explain it, honey.'

'I'll ask my mom. She'll know.'

'I'm sure she will,' muttered Blake.

Blake had pulled up outside a cottage-style house that was nestled against a grassy hillside leading down to the beach. Kristy turned in her seat to look out towards the sea.

'I pass this house every day on my way to work,' she told Blake. 'It's beautiful, isn't it? The view must be fabulous.'

'It is—the whole West End skyline—gorgeous at night. I was talking to Darren. He said you loved this house.'

'Darren? Why? Why would you talk to Darren about this house?'

'It was *you* I was talking about, not the house.'

'Do they have a swing?' asked Denny, trying to see over the hedge.

'Yes, there's a swing in the back garden, on the ocean side. And, Kristy, the house is for sale.'

'It——' She stared at him, his implication sinking in. 'Blake, we weren't going to get into this kind of thing.'

'We're not getting into anything. We're just tourists, looking over the scenery. Would you like to have a look, Denny?' And he had them out of the car, walking up the path, magically producing a key for the front door.

'How'ya get a key if you don't know the people?' Denny asked suspiciously.

'I borrowed it from the people who are selling the house for the owners.' Denny shrugged, not really understanding beyond the word 'borrowed'.

Blake opened the door, holding it for Kristy as Denny dashed in ahead of him. Kristy dropped her eyes from Blake's and followed Denny.

'There's no furn'ture!' Denny wailed, looking around the empty living-room. 'Where's all the furn'ture?'

'Nobody lives here right now, honey.' Kristy dropped her arm around his shoulder and turned him towards the dining-room. 'What you have to do is put furniture in it, in your mind.'

'Like a game? Like Daddy's adventure game on the computer?'

'Just like that.'

'But the rooms in the adventure cave have elves, and snakes.'

Blake chuckled. 'We'll leave out the snakes; and the elves—we'll have to think about the elves. Let's start with this dining-room. What do we do with it, Kristy? With those carpets, and the curtains.'

'A big oak dining-table. You know the kind with the carved legs? White oak.'

Blake nodded approval. 'And carved chairs to match? A couple of captain's chairs for the head and foot of the table?'

'And a sideboard,' Kristy added. 'An antique oak sideboard with a big, bevelled mirror set in the top.'

Denny frowned at the empty room. 'Kristy, could we eat pancakes in here? My mom won't let me eat in the living-room, case I spill on the carpet.'

"We'll treat the carpet,' Blake announced. 'My mother used to get the carpet cleaners to treat our carpet at home with some magical solution, and I can tell you, Denny, I spilled as many glasses of milk as you ever have. Probably more.'

Blake followed Kristy back into the living-room. 'Kristy, how would you furnish this room? A big overstuffed living-room suite, like the one at your place?'

'Wouldn't that be perfect? The Chesterfield facing this window, looking out over the ocean. Blake, just think of a summer evening in this room!'

'Sitting with the patio doors open so the sea breeze could come in. You like being near the ocean, don't you, love? So do I. The sound and sight of the sea seems to give me new life, just like——'

'Like what?' She turned away from the window, looking up at him curiously. 'Like what, Blake?'

'Like you, Kristy. Being around you makes me feel alive again, gives the world new colours.' He looked down at Denny who was tugging at his sleeve. 'What is it, Denny?'

'What kind of colours? Can I see the new colours?'

'Maybe some day. Did you see the swing? Right out there.'

'Can I swing on it, Blake? D'ya think the people'd mind?'

'I'm sure they wouldn't. Here, I'll let you out the patio doors.' He snapped the lock and slid the heavy glass doors back. 'I'll leave them open and you can come back in this way when you're done.'

The house was perfect. She had always been attracted by it, liked the hedge that allowed a passer-by only glimpses of the home within. She had no business going through the rooms with Blake, but she gave in to temptation and let him take her hand and lead her through the rest of the rooms, to the thickly carpeted master bedroom.

'Do you like it?' he asked, his hands on her shoulders as they stood in the doorway to the bedroom.

'It's perfect. I love all the carpet. It makes me want to kick my shoes off and curl my toes into it, it's so thick and soft.'

'Suitable for you, darling. You're always kicking off your shoes. At least here you wouldn't get cold feet.'

She turned to find him searching her face intently. His hands came up to frame her face, his fingers spreading through her hair, tensing against her scalp as he bent slowly towards her. She stared at his lips, hypnotised by anticipation, her own lips parting as his came near.

His lips reached hers in a featherlight touch, brushing against her mouth, then settling to caress her trembling lips. She closed her eyes as his arms came around her, letting the sensation of closeness wash over her.

As his hands moved on her back, she found herself relaxing against his touch, her arms crawling up to hold his head, lacing fingers through his hair and holding his head down against her. When his lips drew away from hers, she tipped her head back and felt his mouth softly making its way along her neck, then nibbling gently against her ear.

His hands could stir her to passion with the slightest motion, but now they held her close, quietly, until their breathing quieted and they were held, cuddled together in each other's arms.

She lifted her head to look at his face. His eyes were half closed, his lips curved in a lazy half-smile.

'Do you like the house, Kristy? Share it with me.'

'No, I—I can't marry you, Blake. I——'

'It doesn't have to be all at once, Kristy. Let's leave marriage out of it for the moment. The idea seems to panic you so much.' His hands were kneading her shoulders, massaging the sudden tenseness away. 'We'll take it one step at a time. Come to Mexico with me. It'll be easier, away from—away from all the everyday details. We'll have time to just be together, get to know each other. Then, when we get back——'

'Blake, I don't think we should. This whole thing scares me. It——'

'When we get back, let's come here. You and I. We could furnish this house together, make it into our home.'

'You mean——What do you mean, Blake? Live together? You and me?'

'Yes. Give it a chance, Kristy. Stop running away. Come away to Mexico with me, then live with me here.'

'Without being married? You want me to live with you without being married?'

'If that's the only way, then yes.'

'I—I couldn't do that, Blake!'

'Why not? You're the liberated lady, free of all the old——'

'That's beside the point! You and I living together, not married! How could I ever face your mother?' And, as he snorted with laughter, 'Stop it! Stop laughing, you idiot! Your mom would be shocked! I couldn't do that to her!'

'I don't know, love. I think my mother might just surprise you. Should I ask her?'

'You've got to be joking! Ask——Don't you dare, Blake Harding! And do you really think living with you would be any less dangerous than marriage? It's not the ceremony I object to, for heaven's sake!'

'What is it, then? Tell me, love.'

'Stop calling me "love"!'

'Make me,' he dared with a devilish grin. 'Try and make me!'

'We should go. Paula must be wondering where we are.'

'All right, coward. Let's go. We'll find Denny and head for home. Maybe he'd like a visit to the Dairy Queen first. We could phone Paula and tell her her darling is in good hands.'

'You're addicted to the Dairy Queen.' She moved quickly away from the bedroom, conscious of Blake walking close behind her.

She couldn't help enjoying his company, having fun as they drove to the Dairy Queen and shared three of the biggest sundaes they could get. But she knew what he was doing. He was trying to seduce her away from her career, to charm her and enchant her and win her away from Point Grey College.

Blake set out to entertain Kristy, to distract her from her pensive mood, then found himself simply relaxing and enjoying being with her.

When they had taken Denny home, Blake started up the stairs with her.

'You're not coming in, Blake.'

'Why not?'

'You know very well why not.'

He shook his head, grinning. 'I've no idea. Tell me.'

'You——Oh, come off it! Being around you is a big risk for any girl who values her freedom.'

'Not any girl, Kristy; just you. And what are you risking? Happiness?'

'Have I told you that you've got an ego the size of a house? You're not coming into my apartment, Blake.'

'Then why don't you come to my place?'

'You don't seriously think that I'm going to do anything so silly?'

'Neutral ground? Dinner downtown?'

'Why don't you just go away?'

'No way, love.'

'I'm not dressed for dinner out. Look at me! Jeans and a sloppy shirt.'

'I'll wait while you get ready.'

'I'm not hungry.'

'We'll go downtown, to the club where Linda's singing. You'd like to see Linda, wouldn't you?'

Kristy was momentarily distracted. 'I can't believe she's really singing. She was such a shy kid——Oh, no, not tonight, Blake. I'd really like to see her, but I don't feel up to noise and dancing tonight. Could we just go walking on the beach instead? I'm probably safer on the beach than on a dance floor with you!'

It had been such a lovely day, Kristy didn't want it to end. When Blake caught at her hand, she let her fingers curl around his.

They walked for hours, stepping around sunbathers, ducking as small children kicked up sand in their play. Blake bought her a hot dog at a kiosk.

'Is this the way you always eat? Hot dogs and ice-cream sundaes?'

'Don't you like it?'

'I love it! My mother would have a fit, but I love it! I want to see the sunset. It's going to be gorgeous over the water with those big white clouds on the horizon.' She grinned at him, feeling a carefree joy she couldn't remember experiencing since those summers back on Saltspring Island.

'Over here, then. Come on.'

'Just a minute. I want to take my sandals off. My feet are killing me!'

'Here, lean on me.' His arm slipped around her waist to support her as she slipped off the sandals and curled her toes in the sand. She leaned against him, not really knowing if she had lost her balance, or if her body was following its own wishes without her consent.

When the sun had faded to pale red in the sky, they remained sitting on the grass, talking easily about everything and nothing, watching the people slowly pack up and leave the beach.

When the talk slowed, Kristy found her eyes dropping closed. It was so relaxing, leaning back on the grassy hillside, feeling Blake close beside her.

'Tired, sleepyhead?' he asked softly, his hand brushing gently against her face.

'Sorry, it must be all the fresh air. I can hardly keep my eyes open.'

Kristy made an effort to wake up, rolling over on the grass, resting her chin in her palms as she tried to see Blake in the dark.

'What's Norm like—your partner?'

'Very serious. He's got a sense of humour, but most people don't realise it. He's tall, about six feet four or so, and married to a tiny girl—I doubt if she's even five feet tall.' Blake laughed. 'They're very much in love, but I think he's terrified of her. When she gets excited, she can really let loose.'

'They sound nice.'

'You'd like them, Kristy. We'll have dinner together some time soon, then you can meet them. I think you and Tina—I don't know if that's really her name, or just a nickname because she's so tiny—you'd enjoy her, Kristy. I could see you two being good friends.'

'Blake, please don't keep making plans for me. It's not going to be that simple. My job——'

'Shush, love,' he urged her. 'We're not arguing tonight. Look at the sunset. How could anyone look at that sunset and feel anything but love?'

They were alone with the sand and the sea, shadowed by darkness, when Blake finally sat up, grasping her hand.

'Come on. You're shivering. I think you're almost asleep. I'll take you home and put you to bed.'

'You're not putting me to bed,' she protested without any heat. Somehow she couldn't feel threatened by him on this lazy evening. She was surprised to realise how exhausted she was. They must have walked miles since leaving Denny at home.

They walked slowly back, his arm around her waist, encouraging her to lean against him as she walked. Her apartment was cool when Blake unlocked the door.

'Be sure you get that lock changed,' he reminded her as he handed the keys back to her. 'Call the locksmith on Monday.'

'Don't lecture me, Blake. I'm too tired to argue.'

'I'll light the fire here. Run yourself a hot bath to relax in, then you're going to sleep.'

'I don't need to relax. I'm so relaxed already that I'm a blob of jelly.'

'You don't look like a blob of jelly.' He smiled slightly, though his eyes remained dark and inscrutable.

'You'd better go, Blake.'

'You keep saying that. I'm not going. I'm going to look after you. You need a little looking after for a change.'

It was so much easier to give in, let him stay.

'Stop fighting,' he urged her softly.

'What are you? A mind reader?'

'Yours is the only mind I care to get into.' His hands were on her arms, drawing her closer, then pushing her down on to the sofa.

She let his hands push her back on to the cushions. Her eyes closed. He lifted one foot and slipped her sandal off. 'You know, I don't think I've ever seen you in real shoes, expect when we went hiking on Saltspring Island. Remember the day you turned up in bare feet to go rockclimbing?'

'You made me go back and put real shoes on. I was furious.' But she had gone. Somehow, Blake always managed to get his way.

He rubbed the sole of her foot, firmly, not tickling. 'You're always wearing sandals, or bare feet.'

'I hate shoes; I always kick them off.'

His strong hands were surprisingly gentle as they rubbed her aching feet.

She rested, content to leave her eyes closed and her ears open to the sounds of Blake moving about her apartment. She smiled when she heard the water running in her bath. Unless she had the energy to oppose him very energetically, she'd be having a hot, relaxing bath within minutes.

'I feel sorry for your mother, Blake,' she murmured when his footsteps came close again.

'Why?'

'I never really thought of it before, but she must have had a terrible time with you. You were always like this, weren't you? Determined to get your own way no matter what anyone said.'

'I suppose,' he admitted. 'But I haven't always had my own way.'

Outside, a siren wailed, then faded. Ambulance, she decided, feeling a fleeting sadness for the anonymous victim. When the ambulance wail faded, the silence seemed total. He started rubbing her feet again, as if he could feel the aching in them from the hours of walking. His hands felt so good. He moved to her lower legs with a firm, massaging motion.

She shifted, thinking of sitting up. 'I should have a cup of coffee. I've got to wake up—I've got marking to do this weekend.

'No, you don't.' He had done something to the

pillows under her head. She should insist, should get up and take charge of her own life. In a moment she would. Just a moment's rest first.

She opened her eyes. Blake's face was very close to hers. She stared up, unable to read the expression in their black depths.

'There's no need to look after me, Blake. I've been looking after myself for a long time.'

'Too long. Close your eyes,' he instructed in that insistent, gentle voice.

She was drifting on a warm tide when firm hands moved her. Her eyes fluttered open again. This was when she should push away, take charge of herself.

She didn't want to.

'Come on, honey.' His hands drew her to her feet. She slumped against him as he slipped his arms under her and lifted her.

His hands were on her, touching her skin now. She glanced down, watching almost dispassionately as he lifted her shirt and pulled it over her head.

'What are you doing?'

'Undressing you. Relax and quit worrying.' He tossed her shirt on to the chair across from them. A moment later, her bra landed on top of the shirt. His face was serious and intent as he finished undressing her.

'Just a hot bath. To relax you muscles. Your legs are so tensed up, you'll be sore tomorrow if we don't do something.'

'I'm too tired.'

With an undertone of humour, he murmured, 'Close your eyes and forget it. I'll do the work.'

'You're laughing at me,' she accused weakly.

'Hush.'

She let her eyes close, let her head drop back against his shoulder as he carried her to the bath. His hands worked firmly, gently, on her aching body. She couldn't remember, even as a child, anyone tending to her like this. He soaped her skin, massaging and caressing it. She closed her eyes again.

When he lifted her out of the bath, she was enveloped in a large, fluffy towel and lifted into his arms again.

'I can walk,'

'No you can't.' His lips brushed against her damp cheek. 'Besides, I'm enjoying this.'

'Are you taking me to bed?'

'I'm *putting* you to bed. There's a difference.'

He lowered her on to the bed, then rubbed the towel gently over her body until she was dry. When he slid the towel away and covered her with her own thick quilt, she missed the touch of his hands on her body.

'Don't stop,' she whispered. 'Don't stop touching me.'

He smoothed her hair back from her forehead. 'We'll take that up another time.'

She opened her eyes slowly, concentrating on his words, not making much sense of them.

'Are you leaving?'

'Not yet. I'm going to sit with you a while.'

It felt good, snuggled under her covers with his hand lightly on her head. She drifted on the edges of sleep until the moment when his hand dropped away from her.

The room was half lit. Blake was a dark silhouette sitting on the edge of her bed. The mattress was lower under his weight. She had rolled towards him in her sleep, throwing her arm across his legs. She could feel the warmth of him under her hand.

Her voice was husky in the darkness.

'Would you like to make love to me?'

'Oh, yes, I would like to.' His hands took charge of

her arm, placing it firmly under the covers again. 'But I'm not going to.'

'Why?' Surely he wouldn't push her away again. When he held her, kissed her, she could always sense his deep need of her. Yet, when she offered herself to him——In her mind, she was back on the lawn outside the Saltspring Island summer home. She was a sixteen-year-old girl, bewildered by Blake's abrupt rejection of all she had offered. She hardly heard his answer.

'The first time I make love to you, that's going to be an experience neither one of us will ever forget. We'll save it for a better time.'

She shook her head weakly against the sheets.

'I want you to—now.' The desire was there, although weak. Mostly she wanted the feel of him touching her, the warmth of his nearness.

'I want you to hold me,' she mumbled. 'I want——'

She didn't know what she wanted. She shook her head, closing her eyes again.

She felt the covers moving against her skin, then the warmth of Blake's body against her. She turned to him as his arms gathered her close.

'Lie still, you witch,' he whispered roughly. 'Just lie still and go to sleep.'

She turned her head, letting her face rest against the smooth cotton of his shirt.

'You'll wrinkle your clothes.' She thought he laughed at that. 'Are we going to sleep?' She felt suddenly quite alert, although she couldn't seem to open her eyes.

'I'm not going to sleep. But you are. Now be quiet, Kristy.'

'You never did tell me why you hit Dave Bentley.' She shifted a little so that his arm fitted more comfortably behind her back. She found his other hand in the darkness under the covers. She curled her fingers into the space inside his strong, warm hand.

His hand clenched, gripping her fingers tightly for a moment. 'It was—you were starting to grow up that year. I'd been trying not to notice. Looking at you that summer, I started wanting things that were impossible, totally impossible. You were fourteen. I was twenty-one.

'Dave was starting to look at you, too, starting to get ideas. That day, up on the hillside, he started talking about you. You were becoming so damned sexy, but so young, so damned vulnerable. I couldn't stand the thought of him touching you.'

'You were protecting me from Dave? That's why you hit him?'

'I don't know how much I was protecting you, or just giving way to possessive jealousy. I told him to stay away from you. I told him if he touched you, I'd——He laughed. He wasn't listening. So I made sure he knew that I meant it.'

She remembered Dave on the ground, staring up at Blake, saying, 'All right. All right! I get the message.' She hadn't seen much of Dave for the rest of the summer. It hadn't occurred to her until now that he had been avoiding her.

'Possessive.' She shook her head, trying to clear the fog from her brain. 'That doesn't make sense. It's not like you. You've always been so controlled, so rational.'

'Except where you're concerned. You're the one who's always been able to get under my skin, making me lose control.'

She was wide awake now. She stared at the darkness of his face next to hers. 'That can't be true.' She was in his arms now. He was holding her naked body under the blankets, but making no move to seduce her.

'Can't it?'

He certainly had hit Dave—the only fight she had

ever seen him in. And the night he first came to her apartment——

'Maybe it's just men called David,' she suggested with a giggle. 'That night you came to my apartment, and David——'

'I was raging jealous.' He had been quiet, but she had seen his eyes, known he was filled with a cold, dangerous anger.

'Why?'

'When I kissed you on Saltspring Island, I knew—I believed there was no one else. If there'd been another man, I thought I would have known when I kissed you.'

He brought her head back down on to his shoulder. 'I knew you were frightened—frightened of loving, I thought—but I didn't expect when I came round here that I'd find a man who thought he had a claim on you. When I found him here, and I could see what was between you, I went a little crazy. I couldn't leave you alone with him here, couldn't go away and let him make love to you.'

'David never mattered.' David had never been able to reach more than the surface of her. He couldn't touch her inner self.

'I stopped being jealous of him once I realised that. Kristy, the day you turned sixteen, you laid your claim on me. Every woman I've ever held in my arms since then, I've ended up comparing with you.'

'It didn't stop you making love to other women.'

'Jealous?'

'Of course not!'

He didn't believe her. He smoothed her hair with his hands, stroked his hand along her side, over the curve of her hip. 'You were far away, gone from my life.' He drew her close against him, his touch gentle and passionless.

Was it true that she had that effect on him? If so,

how could he hold her like this? She twisted in his arms, thought she felt his arm tense as her movement brought his hand across her breast.

She could see his face in the moonlight from the window. He hadn't drawn the curtains, so letting the streetlights and the moon bathe her bedroom in a soft illumination. She watched his face, his eyes watching her.

He was so close, so——She placed a hand gently against his chest, feeling the roughness of his hair through the shirt.

'Kristy,' he groaned as she rubbed her palm where she could feel his male nipples through the shirt. She slipped her fingers through the space between his buttons, fascinated by the feel of his skin, by the expression on his face as she loosened one of the buttons and slipped her whole hand under the cotton fabric.

'Kristy,' he groaned again, his voice thick and hoarse. 'Do you know what you're doing to me, love?' His hands drew her close, his lips finding hers and plundering them in a deep, intimate kiss.

She was drugged by the effect of her hands on Blake's body. Touching him, feeling his response, she found she couldn't stop. Knowing where this was leading, she kept looking for ways to touch his body, to push him to that moment when he finally lost all control and pushed her down, leaned over her and began to make love to her, growling deep in his throat,

'Kristy, darling! Oh, I pray to God that we know what we're doing!' His lips covered hers, demanding everything she could give, his hands finding every sensitive erotic spot on her body until she begged him to take her. Still he inflamed her with his hands and his lips, until she was trembling with need in his arms.

Then his body possessed hers, his kiss covering her cries as he took her to the shared ecstasy of fulfilment, loving her in the soft glow of city lights mixed with moonlight . . .

Later, when they lay spent in each other's arms, she found herself trembling, suddenly cold. He had taken so much from her, drawing a response that left her vulnerable and exposed.

She loved him. She hadn't wanted to love him and she was frightened, knowing she couldn't accept a life with him on his terms, yet terrified she would be unable to walk away from him. She wanted to curl her body into his arms, to sleep with him for ever, yet her own desire filled her with a terror she couldn't understand.

She pushed herself away from him, leaning on one elbow and looking down at his face. She thought he had been asleep, but his eyes opened as she moved, watching her.

'You've got to understand about my career, Blake,' she said suddenly, harshly. She felt him tense, though his face was still and expressionless. 'It's important to me. It's me—a part of me that I can't give up. If I stopped working, tried to make myself into a homemaker——Blake, I'm not good at those things. I'd make a mess of it. And I need my own——My work is part of me. Like my arm, or my hair.'

After a long moment of stillness, his arms slid away from her. 'Quiet, Kristy. Go to sleep.' He pulled her down. His lips brushed hers briefly, almost impersonally, before he settled her head into the hollow of his shoulder. 'Go to sleep. And be sure you get that lock changed next week.'

She lay still, feigning sleep. She slowed her breathing, trying to keep her body relaxed. It seemed an age before he shifted slowly, moving away from her and settling her head on to the pillow, drawing the covers over her as he stood beside the bed.

He stood there for a long moment. She kept her

eyes closed, resisting an urge to hold out her hand, ask him to stay.

When his feet moved softly away, she listened to the sounds of him in the next room. He moved across the living-room, then opened the door.

And he was gone.

CHAPTER NINE

MONDAY was the longest day Kristy could ever remember working through. She saw Jack briefly in the corridor, twice, but he didn't seem to see her.

She learned from Corrine that the interviews ended at noon. If Blake was there, in the boardroom—and he must have been—Kristy saw no sign of him. She waited in her classroom at noon, thinking he might come to ask her to lunch.

Perhaps he didn't want to see her today. Today was the day he would tell the other members of the board that they mustn't select her for Jack's job.

Legally, she probably had a human rights case if Blake prevented her from getting this job, but she knew she could never pursue it. Not against Blake.

When classes ended, Jack was in his office with the door closed, a sign that he did not want to be disturbed. That probably meant that he didn't want to see her yet, didn't want to have to tell her that she wasn't the board's choice.

She half expected that Blake might call, or turn up at her apartment. He might come asking for a ride to night school—only Blake would have the nerve to do that after sabotaging her career.

He didn't call, didn't come to the class at all. She kept glancing at the door of the computer lab, expecting Blake to walk in, but he never came.

He knew how angry she would be over his sabotaging her career. He was staying away, giving her time to get over it. With his wretched invincible confidence, he was certain that she'd come around eventually.

And he was right, damn him! She couldn't pretend to herself any longer. She loved him. She wasn't going to quit her job, but she would probably forgive him for what he had done to her today in that boardroom.

When the students had gone, Kristy let herself out of the building and into the dark, empty car park. She drove through the streets, turning right instead of left, driving past the building on Pine Street.

If she had placed his apartment right in that building, he wasn't home. The windows were all dark, the curtains drawn. She saw no sign of his car, though that didn't mean much as he seldom drove it.

If the lights had been shining through the window, would she have stopped, knocked on his door?

She didn't know. She was afraid to see him again after last night, yet agonisingly disappointed that he hadn't come to her today. She drove back to her own apartment. It was dark, lonely, with no sign of Blake.

She went to bed, terribly conscious of her loneliness.

In the morning she woke early, decided she would phone Blake today if he didn't call her. She drove to work in a somewhat cheerier frame of mind.

Jack called her into his office as soon as she arrived.

'Congratulations, Kristy.'

'What?'

'The job's yours. The board selected you. Unanimously—in a sense.

I've got the job? Me? What do you mean, in a sense?'

'Harding didn't exactly vote for you, of course.'

Of course he hadn't. She had known he wouldn't. But how could he have failed to influence the others? Especially the principal, who would have been so easy to turn against her.

'He explained to us that he's known you since you

were kids. Your families used to be neighbours?'

'Our summer homes. Yes.'

'Well he explained that. Said he hadn't realised you were one of the candidates when he agreed to sit on the interview board. That he couldn't properly cast any vote, but if he could he'd certainly recommend you for the job. That, of all the candidates, you were the only one who had a realistic view of the job; that you had the dedication and ability to ensure that the business department kept up with modern technology.' Jack laughed. 'Kristy, you really should have heard it. Mac was having trouble accepting the idea of a woman director, though he knew you were the best choice. Harding didn't vote for you, exactly, but he proceeded to summarise the qualifications of the other three, tearing them apart in terms of their suitability for the job. Then he abstained from the final selection, but it was a foregone conclusion by then.'

She had to call him, thank him. She had to find out why he'd done that for her.

It was noon before she could get away from her class. She dialled Blake's office. She knew the number off by heart, although she'd only seen it once on a slip of paper—a phone message to call Blake.

An icily efficient voice informed her that Mr Harding was not available. Two hours later—the next time she managed to slip away from her class—the same voice said, 'Mr Harding won't be back today. Could Mr McKay help you?'

'No. No, I'll call back tomorrow. Thank you.'

Kristy cooked salmon steaks and baked potatoes for her dinner with Amanda Harding that night. She was tossing a salad when Amanda knocked on her door.

'Smells lovely, Kristy. How are you, my dear?'

'All right. I'm fine.'

'You look tired. So does Blake. I think you young

people all work too hard. I'm glad he's taking a holiday again. I know he took some time off to go with me to the island this summer, but he didn't seem to be able to relax. That's what you need, Kristy. Are you going to be having a holiday soon?'

'In another week. I'm starting a new job the beginning of October—I've been promoted. Meanwhile, I'll have my holidays.' She stopped, realising that she was chattering almost frantically. 'When—where is Blake going?'

'He's gone.'

'Gone? But how could he? He was here only——Monday morning I know he was at the college.'

Amanda gave her a penetrating look, but went on without commenting on Kristy's tense manner. 'And Monday night he flew to Mexico. I was surprised, too. He was supposed to come to dinner on Sunday. He came, but he was terrible company. I said he'd been overworking and he agreed, said he'd probably take some time off now that the Canning contract was settled. Then he phoned me up yesterday afternoon from the airport and said he'd be in Mexico for a week or two.'

The promotion was his goodbye present to her. She had finally convinced him that her career meant more to her than he did.

Damn him! It wasn't like him to give up so easily. He'd not only given up, he'd disappeared, taken himself to the other end of the continent, out of her reach.

If he hadn't returned by the time she started her holidays, she would follow him. He would be in that village, wouldn't he? The village they had talked about visiting together. Why hadn't he waited, taken her with him?

When the week had passed with no sign from Blake, Kristy decided to phone Amanda. Driving home

Friday night, she planned what she would ask. Casually—no, there was no need for deceit. Amanda had known the night she came to dinner. She hadn't said anything, but her eyes had been worried, concerned. Kristy could just ask, straight out, had Amanda heard from Blake?

Every day, when she came home, she had half expected that Blake would be waiting in her apartment. She couldn't believe he'd really given up that easily. She always tried the doorknob with her hand, somehow certain it would be unlocked. Blake would be inside, waiting for her.

As always, on Friday her door was locked. He wasn't there.

She got her keys out of her purse. She should have accepted Wilma's invitation to dinner. She'd go insane, sitting inside all weekend, waiting. She was afraid to go out, afraid that she might miss a phone call. Mexico might be thousands of miles away, but they did have telephones.

She pulled the key back out of the lock. She must have the wrong key, or have it upside down. No, that was the one. She slid it back in, right side up.

The key didn't fit.

It was the right key, but it didn't fit.

She realised why when she took a closer look at the door. The lock had been changed for a businesslike double lock, the sort that was advertised as burglarproof.

Paula hadn't mentioned any plans to change the locks, but it certainly wasn't a bad idea. She'd love to see Blake come along with his credit card now, planning an easy entry to her apartment, only to find himself outfoxed by a burglarproof lock.

Paula would have the new key for her.

'The what?' Her young landlady looked bewildered at the request. 'What key?'

'My key. My locks have been changed.'

Paula nodded. 'I guessed that. I saw the locksmith's truck here this afternoon. I take it that David's no longer a welcome guest?'

'David doesn't have a key. I've never given anyone a key.' Blake didn't need one. He just pulled his credit card trick. Not that a lock would stop him either. He'd——'What do you mean? Didn't you call the locksmith?'

'No. I thought you had. You didn't? But that's crazy, Kristy. Locksmiths don't go around changing locks at random.' Paula giggled. 'There's no profit in it.'

'Are you sure Dean didn't?'

'Positive. He's in the throes of giving birth to his thesis; reality has ceased to exist for him. I'm hoping it's only temporary, but for the moment you can be sure Dean isn't behind anything as mundane as calling a locksmith.'

'Then it was Blake. He told me to get my locks changed. I didn't, so he's done it himself.'

Blake was here. In Vancouver. He hadn't given up after all. Typical! He couldn't just come to see her. He had to lock her out of her home, prove that he was the one calling the shots.

'I'll get him.' She didn't know how yet, but she wasn't about to take this lying down. She certainly wasn't going to call him, meekly asking for her key.

'Which locksmith, Paula?'

'How would I know. I've never called a locksmith in my life. There must be a hundred of them in Vancouver.'

'What about the truck? It had a name on it, didn't it?'

'I didn't really notice, Kristy. All I saw was the word LOCKSMITH in big letters. I suppose there must have been a company name as well, but I didn't see it.'

'Can I see your phone book?'

That was hopeless. She called the first listing, just in case Blake had chosen the first name in the yellow pages.

She had no way of knowing if it was the right locksmith or not. The man at the other end of the line wasn't giving out confidential information about his customers . He might have done an installation near Kits beach that day, or he might not have. In either case, he wasn't divulging any information about his clients.

If Blake was his client, he'd chosen his man well.

'Why don't you call him?' Paula asked curiously.

'Call Blake? No way. Not when he's sitting there, waiting for me to call. I'll break a window first. Don't worry, I'll pay to get it fixed, but——'

'What's up?' Dean Barnay appeared from the hallway, staggering in from another world. 'Paula, I can't concentrate with all this yakking going on.' He glared at Kristy. 'What's up?'

'My lock's been changed and I can't get in.'

'Paula, why did you change the lock?'

'I didn't. It was——'

'Forget it. I haven't time for this. You realise that my thesis has to be in by Monday. Let Kristy in the inside door and then please keep it quiet around here!'

Paula made a face at his disappearing back. 'When his thesis is finished, that man is going to pamper me until I forgive him,' she told Kristy. 'I only put up with it because I love him—and because he puts up with my bitchy days. What idiots we are, Kristy, not thinking of the inside door.'

The inner door that connected the upstairs apartment to the rest of the house was kept permanently closed. Kristy always used the outside entrance. Even

Denny, when he visited her, came to the outside door.

Virtually everyone had forgotten that the door existed. Except Dean.

The locksmith hadn't forgotten. The inner door was fitted with a sturdy new lock.

'That's crazy,' Paula complained. 'Surely the smith wouldn't change the locks and not leave a key with someone.'

'Blake's got the keys.'

'You're not really going to break a window, are you? The noise is going to upset Dean, and I don't think you should.'

'I won't.'

She wasn't phoning, trying to get through that icy, efficient secretary he had on his switchboard. He'd be expecting a phone call, probably waiting by the telephone with a big grin on his face, and that was another reason for not phoning.

It wasn't much past four o'clock. Kristy's classes had ended at three, but Blake was probably at his office.

She drove around his block looking for a parking spot. Parking. She spent more time looking for parking than she did driving. It occurred to her that Blake's approach of walking or taking public transport in the city was far more practical than her constant frantic searches for parking. Damn him, he probably got where he was going faster, even though he left his car behind most of the time.

God, but he was a maddening man! So determined he was right. So arrogant! He wasn't going to get away with this. When she saw him, she was going to——

There had to be something she could do to make an impression on him, shake him out of his ridiculous self-confidence.

She was never going to find a vacant parking spot. She'd spend all day here. It was past four-thirty now.

Rush hour. No left turn at the traffic lights. Her circles became a complex twisted route.

If she stopped in a bus stop, she'd be towed away for sure. She picked a commercial loading zone.

The door to Harding and McKay's offices swung open with an opulent smoothness that was as silent as it was intimidating. Inside, a luxuriously large reception area was presided over by a receptionist sitting at a computer console.

She looked up from the console with cool, silent query, communicating with one glance that Kristy was not the sort of person normally welcomed in these doors.

Just the kind of secretary Blake would have, smooth and polished, radiating icy control—everything Kristy wasn't.

'Is Mr Harding in?' Kristy resisted the urge to smooth down her hair with her hands. It was futile anyway. She'd never make herself look like this icy madonna.

'You have an appointment?'

'No.' There was no way she was explaining to this woman. 'Tell him Kristy's here.'

The woman stared disapprovingly back at Kristy. 'I'm afraid that——'

'I'll tell him myself.'

'You can't go in there! If you'll just sit down and wait for a moment I'll——'

'I'm in no mood to wait.'

There was no real doubt which door Blake was hiding behind. His name was on the door—an ornate carved nameplate mounted on a carved wooden door. The fact that the door was closed was obviously a signal to his secretary that he wanted privacy.

'Don't open that door!'

The smoothly groomed secretary was beginning to lose her cool, fluttering along beside Kristy, sputtering protests that were becoming progressively less coherent.

'You can't go in there!' she wailed in a final protest as Kristy threw the door open, listening to it hit the stop with a satisfying thud.

Blake was seated behind a massive mahogany desk, his chair turned so that he faced the window and an awesome view of English Bay. He was dressed more formally than she had seen him before, in a dark suit that emphasised his own dark good looks. For a minute he remained sitting, watching her warily, as if he wondered what she was about to do. Then she saw the spark of laughter in his eyes.

'You're a rat!' she flashed at him.

'An ageing male chauvinist pig?' he murmured as he left the big chair behind the desk. 'Make up your mind, dear. Am I a pig or a rat?'

'That doesn't begin to describe you!'

'Sonia, leave us alone please.' Blake's eyes didn't leave Kristy's for a moment.

'Blake—Mr Harding—this woman just walked in and insisted——She wouldn't sit down. She——'

'Thank you, Sonia.' He came close enough to touch Kristy, but his hands stayed at his sides. He was still watching her every minute. He hadn't even glanced at the polished Sonia.

Maybe he knew what he was doing, watching her like that. If she got the chance, she'd do something drastic.

'Leave us now, Sonia. And hold any calls. I don't want to be disturbed.'

'Mr Canning will be here in a few moments.'

'Cancel Canning, or get Norm to deal with it.'

'But——'

Blake ushered Sonia out and firmly closed the door behind her.

'I don't like your secretary!' Kristy moved away,

across the room to where she could look out of the window.

'I have a feeling it's mutual.'

'And you think that's funny? Damn you, Blake! How could you do that—lock me out of my apartment?'

'It was an inspiration. Once I'd thought of it, I couldn't resist.'

'Oh, damn! I know I'm laughing, but it's not funny! I'm so mad at you, I——If you go around behaving like this, how come no one's murdered you yet? No! Keep your hands off me. Why on earth did you lock me out? For what? What's the point?'

'It got you here, didn't it?'

'Don't be so sure that's a good thing. What a bloody nerve! You deserve——'

'What? Can't you——'

'Don't touch me! I'm so mad at you, I could take that computer on your desk and chuck it through the window. All those fancy electronics won't survive a twenty-foot drop.'

'Come on, Kristy.' He was smiling widely now, his eyes sparkling. 'You can do better than that. I saw you sneaking an admiring look at it when you came in. You're far more likely to forget I'm here and start making up to my computer.'

She snorted. 'Give me five minutes with it and I'll scramble your files so you'll never make sense of them again.'

'No you wouldn't.'

'What makes you so sure? If I wanted to, I could.'

'I'm sure you could, but you won't.' He wasn't touching her, but somehow he had manoeuvred her so that she couldn't step back without running into the window—or Blake.

'I want my keys!' she demanded.

'You could try persuading me,' he suggested. 'For

example, you might try a kiss.'

'The hell I will!'

'I've noticed that you're swearing a lot lately.' His hands enclosed her arms, making contact slowly, gently, as if he were edging up on a frightened animal. 'That's not very ladylike, my dear.'

'Maybe I'm not a lady!' She pushed frantically at his hands. 'Let go of me! Get your hands away! Blake, you——'

'You're so beautiful when you're angry.' His voice was oddly hoarse, his hands sliding up her arms again. She twisted against the sensuous attraction of his hard, male hands on the bare skin of her arms. 'You're always so beautiful.'

'I'm not. You know I'm not. If you want beauty, go through the door. Your secretary——'

'Is a cold woman. Efficient, granted, but comparing her to you is like comparing an icicle to the flame. You're alive, Kristy, passionately—'

'Passionately angry! For heaven's sake, Blake, why do you work so hard at making me angry? Is that what you want? Fighting and spitting?'

His hands hardened on her arms, drawing her against him.

She was hypnotised as much by the deep darkness of his eyes as by the harsh grip of his hands on her.

The buzz of a telephone invaded the sudden silence.

'Your phone's ringing,' Kristy announced shrilly.

'Let it ring,' he growled as he drew her still closer. She was frozen in his arms, feeling the tremendous male strength of him. He bent his head to hers and took her lips with a hard possessiveness.

She did try to keep her eyes open, to maintain some kind of frozen distance from the arms that were sliding around to her back, the fingers spreading to trace every nerve along her spine . . . up to the nape of her neck where his fingers spread through her hair in a sensuous massage . . . down to the small of her back where his touch made her body arch in a tormented reaction that brought her into shuddering contact with his hard maleness . . .

Something sharp was pressed against her hip. Something in his pocket.

When his lips drew away from her she took a deep, ragged breath. She found that his grip had softened enough for her to draw back.

'I want my keys.' Her voice was uncomfortably breathless.

He removed a small key ring from his pocket and placed it in her hand.

'Front door . . . back door.'

She glared up at him. 'Don't you usually get two keys for each lock?'

'I'll look after the others.' He spoke absently, his eyes tracing the lines of her body, telling her his thoughts in no uncertain terms.

'Give me those keys!'

'No way, my dear. You can't keep me away by locking doors.'

'You have to have it your own way, don't you? You unprincipled——Come to think of it, how did the locksmith get into my apartment to change the locks? Surely a bonded locksmith isn't going to break in?'

'He might. If the owner of the apartment had lost his key.'

'And you said you were the owner?'

'As a matter of fact, I didn't have to. I gave him a key.'

'You——How could you have—you took the spare key from my kitchen!'

'It was an irresistible temptation.'

'You and your irresistible temptations! And you didn't stop to think you had no right? That I didn't want you to have a key? No one's ever had a key to my apartment!'

'I do. Now.' He moved around to the far side of his desk, began moving some of the papers into a side drawer. The same drawer she used, she thought irrelevantly. 'Let's go to dinner. There's a nice place just across the way.'

'Has it never occurred to you that you can't have everything your own way? Have you never heard of compromise?'

His eyes fastened on hers, holding her gaze with an uncomfortable intensity. 'Offer me a compromise, I'm listening.'

The anger drained out of her. 'I——You're supposed to be in Mexico. Your mother said you went to Mexico.'

'I came back.'

'Couldn't you have just phoned? You could have called and asked me to dinner like a normal person.'

'You might have said no, or hung up on me. This seemed a surer way.'

'Give me my keys, the second set.' That wouldn't stop him for long. It would be only a momentary victory. 'And leave me alone.'

'Come on, Kristy! That's not exactly a compromise.'

Compromise. Would he compromise? She didn't want to remember how his hands felt on her body, how his hardness could mould her female softness. A wave of shuddering weakness passed through the centre of her, leaving her legs trembling.

'I want the keys, all the keys.'

'Have you eaten?'

'Will you quit changing the subject? I want the keys.'

'I don't see how you can be rational when you're hungry. I know I can't. Let's go and have dinner, then we can talk.'

'I don't want to have dinner! I'm not dressed for going out. I just——' She stopped. Was it possible that he was nervous?

'Then let's stay in. Personally, I'd far rather have you to myself than share you with the patrons of a crowded restaurant. I'll order dinner in to my apartment, then we'll——'

'First you should give me my keys.'

'I'm not prepared to give them to you on your terms.' He was toying with a stapler on the desk, and again she couldn't help wondering if he was as confident as he seemed.

'Are you saying you might agree to give them to me on some other terms?'

'I'm open to suggestions.'

Compromise. What compromise? Would he still want her to give up her job? One thing was certain. He wouldn't hand over the other set of keys until he was ready—if he was ever ready.

'Dinner? Will you promise——'

'No.' His voice was so low she couldn't be sure what he had said until he went on. 'I'm not making any promises I can't keep.

A totally uncontrollable man. She had to be crazy to allow herself even another minute in his presence. If she weren't so hungry. She had just realised that this trembly feeling in her limbs had to be mostly hunger.

'There's your phone again. Are you going to answer it?'

He shook his head. 'I'll have to have a talk with that girl. I did say no calls.'

'It'll be your Mr Canning. You'd better see him.'

'Canning is not nearly as important to me as you are.'

'My father——'

'I am not your father, Kristy. The only thing we

have in common is a business connection with Canning.'

'What if you lose him as a client? He might not like being stood up.'

'I've looked after his interests pretty well. I doubt if he'll go elsewhere. If he does, it's not the end of the world.'

'Don't you care?' She reached past him to pick up the ringing telephone.

'He'll be out in a minute,' she told an astounded Sonia before Blake took the receiver from her hand and hung it up.

'Has it occurred to you that some of our most important conversations get interrupted by the telephone?'

'It's a good thing; the interruptions distract you. If I'm lucky, you'll get distracted enough to give me an advantage. These aren't conversations we're having —they're fights.'

'Arguments, not fights. An argument is a healthy difference of opinion. A fight is when two people work at hurting each other.'

'And you call this a healthy difference?'

'That's what it is.' He grinned. 'One of these days, we'll be making love, not war. Just like we did last——'

'Don't count on it. You can't win every battle.'

'I'll win this one. I can't give up until I do.' He took her hand in his, turning it to stare at her palm.

'Are you going to tell me my future?'

'I've already told you, you're going to marry a tall, dark man. That's your future, but first let's deal with the present. What are you going to do while I get rid of Canning? That'll take me about five minutes. Then you're having dinner with me.'

It wouldn't do to let him have his way too easily, but she didn't want to fight him, at least not about dinner. 'I'll go home to shower and change. Give me an hour.'

'Before you go . . . ' He was leaning against his desk. He grasped her other hand and pulled gently. When she was close to him, her breasts brushing against the white of his shirt, he stared at her for a long moment. Her hands trembled in his. She started to pull away to conceal her inner reaction to his nearness.

He shook his head slightly, locking her eyes with his. His face moved slowly closer to her. She could feel his breath against her face long seconds before his lips reached hers.

Even later, standing under the pounding spray of a cold shower, her lips still tingled from the burning kiss he had pressed on them before letting her go.

CHAPTER TEN

KRISTY chose a filmy blue dress from her wardrobe. She had worn it to a wedding once, but it was just as suitable for a dinner date.

When she looked in the mirror, her red hair glistened like a cloud of flame against the dark navy of the dress. She tried to see herself through his eyes. He'd like the way the dress hinted at the curves below, the drape of fabric at her neckline crossing over just at the point where her breasts began to swell.

Her father would have stared at her cloud of hair with disapproval, but Blake would look at it with that flame in his eyes. When he looked at her like that, she felt that he had touched her intimately.

'Lady, I hope you know what you're doing,' she told her image in the mirror. The image stared back, eyes wide and cloudy, lips parted. The look of a woman waiting for her lover.

The bell rang at two minutes before seven.

This was the first time she had gone to her door knowing he would be waiting for her on the other side.

He seemed taller than ever, filling her doorway, stepping inside as if he had a right here. His hair showed signs of dampness from the shower he had just taken. Earlier, she had noticed the faint shadow of his beard. It was gone now. She smelled the familiar scent of his aftershave as he stepped close to her, felt a strong urge to reach out and touch his smoothly shaven cheek.

She rubbed the palms of her hands against her skirt.

'You're very beautiful tonight.' His eyes were on her face, her hair. They traced down the V of her neckline.

'Am I?'

He laughed softly, 'You know you are. Ready?'

'I'll just get my bag.' She picked up her keys from the telephone table, slipped them into her bag.

Keys.

She met his eyes across the room. He was waiting for her to ask. Deliberately, she snapped her bag closed and slipped the strap over her shoulder. He opened the door and she stepped past, tensed, knowing he would touch her.

He turned back to the door, using that other key to make sure the door was locked.

She expected his hand at her waist as he walked down the steps at her side. She was tensed, waiting for a touch that didn't come.

'We're making progress,' he told her as he opened the passenger door for her. He checked that her skirt was clear of the door before he closed it.

'Are we?'

She watched him walking around the front of the car. He looked very pleased with himself.

His car started with a muted roar the instant he turned the key. He had his hands on the wheel, his eyes forward as if he were about to start driving, when he asked.

'Do you have any idea how badly I want to touch you?'

'Then why haven't you?'

'You said you wanted dinner.' His eyes met hers and they both laughed as he set the car into motion.

He handled the city traffic with the same cool control he applied to everything. Almost everything, she corrected herself, remembering the uncertainty she had seen in his eyes earlier.

'Why did you say we're making progress? Because I didn't ask for my second set of keys yet?'

'You came home and got ready. You waited for me instead of disappearing.'

'Did you think I would run away?'

'I didn't know.'

'I said I'd go out with you. You're the one who did the disappearing act, running away to Mexico.'

He nodded, acknowledging that, but not explaining beyond saying, 'But I came back.'

'With a bang! Locking me out of my apartment! Where are you taking me now? Why are we on the freeway?'

'I was going to take you out to a fancy restaurant, but it didn't seem like the right thing. I thought we'd go back to the place we started this.'

'Back to——You mean Saltspring Island?'

'Where else?'

She fell silent, suddenly nervous at the thought of Saltspring Island, its magic and the humiliating memory of Blake's rejection of her.

'Are we catching the ferry? Do they run this late?'

'We're flying.'

He stopped his car at a small airfield on the outskirts of the metropolitan area.

'I lease the plane from this flying club every summer,' he explained. 'It's amphibious—it has both floats for water landing, and wheels.'

'I know what amphibious means.'

'Do you?' He grinned. 'I'm trying to fill in your silences. Come on, love. I've got a picnic basket in the back. Let's fly away. Ten minutes from now we'll be far away from the rest of the world!'

'I've never been in a small plane before.'

'Trust me. I'll get you back down safely.'

'How long will it take?'

'We'll be there in half an hour.'

A picnic dinner at the Harding summer home. She closed her eyes briefly, seeing the fire crackling, herself and Blake sitting on the bearskin rug in the warmth. Later, they could walk down to the water, perhaps even swim in the moonlight if the night seemed warm enough.

She climbed into the plane, let him fasten her seatbelt, and found herself watching him as he concentrated on running the plane down the grass runway.

He seemed to control the plane easily, without any tension or worry, but giving it all his attention. The aircraft responded to his touch, lifting off the ground and climbing smoothly until Kristy could look down at the patchwork quilt of the farms that crowded the city outskirts.

When she looked away, she could still see his face, even the small scar on his cheek. The scar hadn't been there twelve years ago. Later, she would ask him how it had happened.

Later—

How could they ever work out a relationship, any kind of relationship? It was impossible, and even if—what if they did, somehow, and she told him she loved him, opened herself and—what if he decided she wasn't the girl he thought he loved?

Blake called Vancouver airport and talked with the air traffic controller for a moment, then they were flying over the water, doing a scenic tour of the Gulf Islands.

Kristy spotted the familiar summer homes as Blake started to circle for a landing. 'I've never seen it from the air before. Look at the Hankensons'—I didn't realise their hedge spelled out their name from the air!'

'It didn't always. I took Abe up for a ride a few years ago and he got the idea. Every year he gets me to take him up again and see how it's progressing.'

The sun was starting to colour the western sky red as Blake taxied the small plane over to the float at the foot of his cottage.

Kristy waited until he opened the door for her, then held her skirt out of the way as she climbed out on to the wharf. 'It's getting dark. How will we get back?'

'We don't need to go back tonight, do we?'

'No, but——'

'You can always stay at your mother's place, if you want to.'

This was a mistake, laying herself open to him, letting him in to where he had ultimate power to hurt her. 'Blake, I don't—let's go back. There's time, isn't there? A restaurant would be——'

'Surely you don't want to play it safe all your life?' He was looking down at her, holding the door open for her. He hadn't touched her yet. 'Scared, Kristy?'

'Yes.'

'It'll be all right.' His hand found her waist with a gentle urging. 'Trust me.'

'We're not climbing a mountain, Blake.'

'I won't hurt you, Kristy.'

'That's not what this is about.'

'Isn't it?'

Silently, she went ahead of him into the house.

'Unpack the basket while I get a fire going,' he said, as if he'd seen her mental image of the two of them in front of the fire.

The food was superb—a succulent seafood salad, followed by irresistibly rich pastries that had them licking the sugar coating from their fingers when the last one had disappeared.

'My mother would have a fit about this. Last time I had lunch with her she lectured me about eating fish and chips.'

'How's her office system going?'

'I've got a system chart roughed out. The best thing

for her would be dBASE. I designed a system on that
assumption, but I've got an ominous feeling she'll
expect me to do the programming for her. It wouldn't
be that hard, but it's probably a month's work to get
it up and working without any bugs. I've got holidays
coming up, so I guess I could do it then.'

'Have you got the proposal typed up for her?'

'Not yet.'

'Then give me the system specifications. I'll get
Sonia to type them up and you can hand it over to
your mother. Tell her all she has to do is buy the
equipment and hand the specs to a programmer.'

'She'll tell me she hasn't a clue how to arrange it
all, and I'll land up doing it anyway.'

'Outflank her before she gets to it. Call up the
hardware dealer and give him a copy of the system
description. Give your mother a list of programmers,
or even choose a programmer for her. Then leave her
on her own.'

'I've got students—ex-students—who could do the
programming job,' she realised. 'It isn't that Mother
minds so much paying for the job—at least I don't
think so—but she doesn't want to be bothered with
the details. I wouldn't want to make her angry with
me.'

'You're going to knock yourself out if you try to
do the whole job for her. She won't appreciate it
anyway. She's using you, Kristy.'

'I know, but——Could you really get them typed?
My notes might be a bit hard to decipher.'

'I'll get them done on the word processor in draft.
Then you can mark any changes you want.'

Tempting, to hand over the notes, get this job for
her mother off her back. She could do it herself,
but—she met his eyes across the table. The food was
almost gone. He was pouring a drink from an insu-
lated silver jug.

Later, he would close the space between them. His eyes touched her now with only a shadow of the heat that his hands would hold, but she had to work at her breathing. Her chest had formed a tight band, squeezing her breath out.

'Blake, you and I—it won't work.'

'Stop fighting yourself and relax. We can work out the details of our relationship later.'

'We don't have a relationship.'

'Do you really believe that?'

'No, but——'

'Stop there. Don't spoil it.'

She caught the aroma of Swiss chocolate as he handed her the steaming cup. The thick creamy liquid slid down her throat as she sipped.

'Blake, why did you recommend me for Jack's job?'

'I didn't. I withdrew from the board.'

'I know what you did. Jack told me about it. Technically, you withdrew, but first you tore apart the other applicants. And why did you go away? I tried to call you, to thank you—to ask you why you did it. That cold-blooded secretary of yours wouldn't tell me a thing. Your mother told me you'd gone to Mexico. Why?'

'I had to do some thinking. You'd given me a lot to think about.'

He came around the table and took her hand in his own. He tugged gently and she was on her feet, facing him. He led her over to the sofa in front of the fire, pushed her gently down, following to sit with his arm behind her. If she leaned back at all, her head would rest on his arm.

'I should never have been involved in those interviews, Kristy. If I'd known you were applying when they asked me, I'd have stepped down. But when you told me, and I realised the position I was in, I wasn't thinking very clearly. I wanted you so, and you kept pushing me away, running. You were using your career as a barrier between us. I'd thought of it that way myself, that you had to quit working, as if you couldn't love both me and your work. I thought if the job wasn't there, you'd see me more clearly. There's always been something between us; you can't deny that, Kristy.'

She shook her head silently.

'You deserved the job. Old Mac couldn't see the issue clearly for his own outmoded prejudices.'

'Outmoded prejudices! You're not in any position to speak about outmoded ideas. You've been determined the only role for a woman is keeping house, looking after babies. You see your mother as the ideal woman. Don't get me wrong, I love your mother, but I'm not the same as she is. I tried for my father. When we were living in Toronto, I tried to——'

'Shh, Kristy, I admit to it all. That's why I had to go away for a few days, to take a good look at myself, and you. And at the interview evaluation. Whatever I wanted, or thought I wanted, I couldn't deny that you were very good at your job. You were certainly the best candidate.'

'Then surely, if you mean that, you must see that it's impossible—you and I?

'Why?'

Because he wanted children and she wasn't sure if she could handle motherhood and her job. Because she loved him and she wasn't sure if she could handle his pushing her away again.

'There's something you're forgetting.'

'What?'

'This,' He cupped her head loosely with his fingers laced through her hair. His eyes were on her lips as his mouth moved closer.

When his touch came, it was the merest feathering of his lips against hers. He traced the shape of her mouth with his own, brushing slowly back and forth until her own lips parted and her tongue slipped out unconsciously to wet them.

He didn't take advantage of this sign of her surrender, but began an erotic exploration of her face, kissing her eyelids, her forehead, her ears, and the smoothness of her throat.

His hands were exploring her scalp through the thick curls, holding her head for the soft caress of his mouth. He drew his lips slowly closer to hers.

Her mouth was trembling in response long before his kiss covered it in a deep, drugging promise of what was to come.

He touched only her face and her hair, yet her whole body was trembling. Her fingers curled into her palms, aching to touch him. In a moment she would. She would reach out with her fingertips to find the smooth maleness of his face, the crispness of his dark hair.

She shuddered as his lips tasted deeply of hers before drawing away. Her hands fluttered up in protest as she lost his touch.

She found his eyes on her face, a question in them deeper than she could answer. He had always asked for more than she could give. She stared back at him, anger growing at her own fears.

'We shouldn't do this, Blake. How can I convince you that it won't work?'

His fingers tightened on her scalp, as if he were about to pull her against him for a hard, demanding kiss. 'Stay with me tonight, darling.' He moved one hand to her shoulder, stroking her arm through the silky fabric.

'How will that prove it won't work?'

'I don't know.' His laughter was a breath against her cheek. 'But you could try.'

It was the needs of her womanly body sending the

blood racing and pounding. It was a physical thing, her head dropping back, her eyes closing, her hands finding his dark, shiny-crisp hair and tangling in it to pull his mouth hard against hers.

'Kristy,' he groaned against her lips as he took them again, his hands slipping down over the filmy fabric. As he stroked the curves of her back, she shuddered and arched against him, drawing herself close with her arms, holding his head as he dropped his lips to the deep V of her dress. 'So beautiful,' he murmured huskily against the white skin he found there. His lips touched and she felt her breasts growing full and hard under the fabric of the dress. In a moment he would touch there. In her mind she felt his hands covering the hard swelling of her breasts, his lips touching the aroused nipples. Her body twisted against his, needing more than the muted contact of skin through too many layers of clothes.

'Let me make love to you again, darling,' he whispered, his hands spreading on her back, fingers curving until they almost touched the soft beginnings of her breasts. He lifted his head and stared deep into her eyes as he moulded her body against his. She wanted to drown in those eyes. She felt his largeness overpowering her with an irresistible surge of emotion that demanded her own surrender.

She wanted his hands on her skin, touching her, drawing the fire. The fire was surging in her veins. His hands moved to her hips, holding her against the hard evidence of his own passion. She felt herself going dizzy, drowning in the depths of those deep, dark eyes.

'Kristy? Darling, what is it?' He let her body drop back against the cushions, his hands on her face now, his lips testing the beginnings of tears on her cheeks. 'Darling?'

If she could just keep from asking, begging, showing him the the depths of her need of him. He read something from her eyes. His hands were gentle on her face, his lips soothing and passionless on hers.

'It's all right. It's all right, darling.' He kissed her eyelids. She had to close her eyes.

He was lifting her in his arms, carrying her down the hallway, away from the fire. Her eyes fluttered when he lowered her gently onto the bed. 'It's all right,' he repeated. His lips covered hers in a gentle, undemanding kiss.

But the need was there, inside, surging for release. She shuddered, knowing she couldn't stop herself, didn't even want to.

'I get carried away,' he was murmuring, drawing her body against his on the big bed. 'Shush. Just let me hold you. I know I was—I won't——If you only knew what you do to me.' She opened her lips to let his mouth take hers. His lips touched hers gently. She trembled, needing so much more.

'I get carried away. I don't mean to, Kristy. I know you need time, but whenever I touch you it's like I'm back under the trees here with you in my arms. I needed you so badly that night. You were so damned beautiful, so desirable. When I feel you in my arms, it's like——I've been waiting all these years, needing you. The other night, in your apartment, I know I shouldn't have made love to you. The time wasn't right, but when you touched me, I—I couldn't wait any longer, darling.'

'The night of my sixteenth birthday you pushed me away, told me to get away from you. You said the last thing you wanted was to end up married to me, with me expecting your child.'

'I don't know what words I said, but you know why—you had to know.'

'Yes,' she whispered. 'I knew. It was me. It was all right at first, but when you realised how much, how badly, I needed you——I shouldn't have clung so. It made you feel trapped, smothered. You had to——'

'Kristy.' His hands clenched painfully on her arms. 'Surely, you knew. My God, woman! If you didn't realise then, surely later, when you were older. Have you any idea how young you were? Sixteen. Just sixteen!

'You were a child. You didn't look like a child; you surely didn't feel like a child. You'd been under my skin, in my blood for a couple of years by then—your child body turning woman, and you. I was dreaming about you night and day. Not the sort of dreams any man should be having about a girl who isn't even at the age of consent.

'I knew it was wrong, but I was managing to keep myself under control. I couldn't stay away from you that summer, but I took you up mountains, on hikes across the island, instead of taking you where I wanted to—into my bed. Sometimes I thought I'd go nuts, throw everything over and just take you. There was a girl—I don't remember her name, but I tried my damnedest to forget the woman part of you. It didn't work. She wasn't anything like you—no one ever could be. I can't even remember now what she looked like.'

'Her name was Sheila. And she was beautiful.'

'Was she? She was twenty-one. I remember that. It seemed important at the time. It didn't work, though. I'd close my eyes and have this redhead in my arms, then open them again to find I'd lost you.

'You were going away. I wanted to take you and make you mine, keep you with me. The whole thing was impossible. You were so young, not even finished high school, not finished being a child.'

'I wasn't that much of a child. I loved you, Blake.'

'You were going though a bad time. Your parents were breaking up. You were about to be moved three thousand miles across the country to a strange city.

You may not have realised it, but you were frightened and lonely. And you were still half child. There was nothing I could say, nothing I could do to help. Except keep in contact. I thought I'd get to Toronto once or twice in the next year, just to keep tabs on you and, well, wait for you to do some growing up.

'Then, the night of your birthday—you were incredibly beautiful that night. Your hair was like it is now, shorter, but that same glorious cloud of soft flame. When you asked me to dance, I should have done something to stop it, but I just couldn't. I wanted you in my arms so badly.

'If I'd been honest with myself, I'd have admitted that going outside with you could only end one way. I told myself we'd just walk. I'd hold your hand and maybe at the end I'd give you a kiss—a very chaste kiss.

'I don't even know how it happened. You were in my arms and I wasn't even trying to remember you were just a child. Your skin was so smooth, I couldn't seem to stop touching it, kissing it.' His hands were stroking now, feeling the warm flesh of her upper arms.

'You did stop. When I was begging you to love me, you stopped. You told me to get away from you, to——'

'I—I was seducing a child! Legally, what I was doing—what I was about to do—was statutory rape! And if I hadn't got my hands off you in a very short time, nothing could have stopped me. You said you wanted me, but you had no idea. There could have been a child!'

'I wouldn't have minded.' She had told him that, almost begged him. 'I guess you didn't want children then.'

'I didn't want you to find yourself sixteen and pregnant, trapped into marrying a man you didn't love because you'd reached out for comfort in a moment of loneliness. I wanted you a woman, and loving me. I know I made a mess of it, but I had to get away. I thought in the morning, in broad daylight, I could talk to you.'

The next morning she had sent a message down to say she didn't want to see him. Then she had gone away, left with the father who had never been able to love her enough.

'What would you have said, if I'd see you that morning?'

His hand traced down her arm, slipped on to her hip and followed the curve to her thigh. 'I don't know, exactly. I was young, too, Kristy. I knew what you did to me, but I'd really no idea how I should deal with you, what to say. If you'd been a few years older—I was afraid of doing too much. I didn't want to trap you into something you'd regret later, but I wanted you to know I'd be around.'

It would have been something to hold on to during the lonely year that followed. They could have written letters. He could have been the secret lover of her fantasies, until she was old enough for him to look on her as a woman.

'You never wrote. You never came to Toronto.'

'You said you didn't want to see me. I believed you.'

'What's changed now? I've been asking you to leave me alone, but you keep coming. You won't give up. You've made chaos of my nice tidy life. You've broken into my apartment, stolen my keys, changed my locks. You terrified poor David!'

'I'm not sorry about David. As for the rest, I'm older now. I'm not nearly so easy to discourage. I was determined to make you mine this time.'

'Determined? That's the understatement of the year!'

'And you were never meant to have a tidy life. It's totally out of character.'

'You only think that because of my red hair.'

'The fire's not just in your hair.' He stroked it back, lifting the curls away from her neck, letting them flow through his fingers. 'I love you, Kristy. I think that if you let yourself, you could love me, too. I don't know how many times I've tried to forget you, darling. Other women——It just never works.'

'Have you had other women here?' She was watching him now, wondering. Was there any other woman he thought of—compared her to—when he kissed her?

'Not here, never. That's why I wanted to bring you here—one of the reasons—and to finish what we started all those years ago.'

He took her face in his hands, dropping a gentle kiss on her nose. She lifted her lips to find his, but he had settled her head against his shoulder. 'I think your image is burned into my brain. When I found you again on Saltspring Island, you were older, more beautiful even than before, but you were the woman who'd been waking me up at night for years, with empty arms, in an empty bed.'

'You set this up tonight—the keys, the dinner invitation. All along you meant to get me here, not out to a restaurant.'

'Yes.'

'And once you got me here, you meant to seduce me, to——'

'To make love to you again—yes.'

She propped herself up on an elbow. Looking down into his eyes, she found their black depths held uncertainty. Blake, uncertain?

'Have you changed your mind?' Her voice was suddenly hoarse. She wanted to tell him, to ask him, but she was frightened to speak the words in her mind. She licked her lips. 'I hope you haven't.'

He shifted abruptly. She found herself lying on her back, staring up at Blake as he demanded, 'What did you say?'

'Why do I have to say it?'

'Please, Kristy.'

'You said you'd go slow, not rush me. I—I don't want you to go slow. I want——I need you.'

His lips covered hers, taking the words in a long kiss that left her clinging to him. Then he began to love her with every part of his body.

He slipped her clothes gently away, stroking her skin to fever pitch, sending the world spinning, driving her finally past the point where she had any control left. Her hands urged him on, needing his need of her . . .

Some time in the dark hours of the night, Kristy woke. She felt none of the confusion of waking in a strange bed. Blake's length was warm against her back, his arm curved around her, holding her against him with a large hand on her midriff.

A few hours ago, his hands had taught her body more about the joys of loving than she had ever believed possible. 'I love you,' he had told her, again and again, as her body made the ultimate female surrender to his.

'I love you,' she had answered silently in her mind.

She hadn't said the words. Had that kept her safe? Could she leave now, slip away from the arms that had held her secure all night?

Years ago, when she was a child, she had run away from loving Blake. If she was going to run again it should be now, while he slept.

She moved slowly, heart thundering, letting his arm slip slowly off her body, easing herself off the bed carefully, making no sudden motion.

She could gather her clothes in the moonlight that came from the window and be gone, quickly. Next door, at her mother's empty cottage, she would be safer. That was what she should do if she wanted—

She went to the window. Blake lay watching her, seeing her beautiful body outlined in silhouette. He wanted to go to her, to take her in his arms and demand that she stay, love him, be his for ever.

But if she was going to go away now, after last night, he didn't think he could stop her. Perhaps he should go to her now, tell her——

What could he tell her that she didn't already know? He had given her his love, his vulnerability. He could do nothing now except to wait, and hope.

She could see the lights from the far side of the bay glistening across the water. Below the window, dark shadows seemed to invite a moonlit walk through the trees.

She had no idea what time it was. Very late, probably, but time didn't seem to matter here.

There was a world outside the island. A million or so people only a few miles away. Her career.

And Blake was here, inside this room—Blake, and the risks of loving. She turned away from the window and walked slowly back to the bed. She sat beside him. Had he been awake all this time, watching her with those deep eyes?

'I love you,' she whispered.

He took her hand, holding it carefully, as if he were nervous she might be damaged from the touch. 'You make it sound like a penalty.'

'I'm afraid. It frightens me.'

'It scares me, too.'

'You? What could you be frightened of?'

'Of loving you, and having you walk away, out of my life.'

'I never thought—you never seemed to need anyone. You were so sure of yourself.'

'I need you. Without you, I'm only half alive. When you're with me, life has sparkle, fire. I told you that before.' He slipped his fingers through her hair, drawing her down for the feather-light touch of his kiss. 'I've got something for you.' He reached across to the bedside table. She heard the clink of keys.

'Why? Why are you giving them to me now? These aren't my keys, Blake. What?'

'House keys. The house we looked at. I want—you know what I want, but—it had to be your decision. We'll do it your way, however you want it.'

She stared down at the keys. 'You want a wife. Children.'

'I want you, Kristy. As you said, if I want a housekeeper, I can put an ad in the paper.'

'You should have children. That's important to you.'

'I don't want children nearly as much as I want you in my life. On any terms you want, Kristy. This job is important to you. All right. But don't leave me.'

She touched his face, traced the hard lines of his jaw where the rough beginnings of a beard had grown. He caught her hand against his cheek and held it there. 'Blake, I do want to have your child. I don't know how I'd be. I don't know much about being a mother, but——'

'Come here.' He shifted to make room for her beside him under the covers. When she was back in his arms where she belonged, he told her, 'We'll take one thing at a time. Right now, you and I. And the house. Would you like to live in that house with me, Kristy?'

'Yes,' she whispered. 'I've been dreaming about that, but—Blake, if my working really matters——'

'Kristy, don't say it. I'm not asking you to give up

your career. I want to share your life with you, not
turn it into a big sacrifice. If you do want children,
that doesn't mean you have to stop working. You'll
have help, you know. There's no reason why I can't
ease off at work, take more time off. And there's my
mother. She'd love nothing better than to help out
with her grandchildren.'

She slipped her arms around him. He was so warm,
so pleasantly firm against her softness. She could feel
him reacting to her nearness, knew that in a moment
there would be no need for words. She moved her
hand against him. 'You'd better be careful, darling,'
she warned as she brushed her lips against his throat.
'They're likely to throw you out of the male chauvinists' union if you make offers like that.'

He turned his head to catch her lips. She let her
hand slide down across his abdomen. His kiss became
hard and demanding. When his mouth left hers, she
was trembling with desire.

'Love me, Blake,' she pleaded on a whisper.

And he did.

The passionate saga
that began with SARAH continues in the compelling,
unforgettable story of

MAURA SEGER

In the aftermath of the Civil War, a divided nation—and two
tempestuous hearts—struggle to become one.

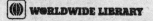

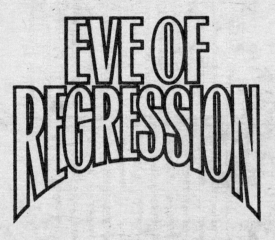

**A soaring novel of passion and destiny
as magnificent as the mighty redwoods.**

REDWOOD EMPIRE

A.E. MAXWELL

He could offer her the priceless gift of security but could not erase the
sweet agony of desire that ruled her days and tormented her nights.

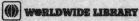 **WORLDWIDE LIBRARY**

RED-1